The Bad Guy

A Novel by Steven Cappetta

Flying
Sasquatch
Publishing

Flying Sasquatch Publishing - First Edition

ISBN: 978-1-7321467-0-9

Cover design by Thuy Hahn Tran

ACKNOWLEDGMENTS

I would like to thank everyone who provided their time and support to make this book possible.

Thank you to my mom, Rebecca, and grandma, Alice, for being my first beta readers and editors. Thank you both for the support and time to make my first book a reality.

Also, a special thanks to Thuy Hanh Tran for the beautiful design cover art.

There are no heroes amongst thieves

CHAPTER 1

Most families are starting to gather together in the warmth of their homes with anticipation of the holiday that is soon to come. Many will relax around a cozy fire and recite stories and memories of years past. The children will laugh and giggle at humorous tales as the heat from the crackling logs in the fireplace evoke a sense of peace. The hint of cinnamon in the air adds to such an experience of contentment that provides a brief respite from the hardships of life and the cold, sullen world that lay beyond the brick walls. My Christmas Eve will not be enjoyed in those comfortable surroundings celebrating the holidays, but instead, be spent out in the frigid December weather where carefully planned and demanding work still has to be done.

***

I glance at the time posted on the dashboard. The boxed, lighted green numbers show 2:23 p.m. I still have plenty of time before we will start. In fact, I may arrive somewhat earlier than I am supposed to, but not too early to affect the plan.

The bleak environment must have sucked all cheerfulness out of the holiday spirit today. The sun did not rise this morning, but instead, hides behind the dull, gray clouds that

1

shadow the earth's surface. The tall, black trees that loom overhead sway with the stiff breeze that gusts through the pine needles adorning each branch. Though I cannot feel the air through the windshield, the view outside makes my skin shiver. It does not matter how heavy a coat one would put on today. The chill outside will attack the body through the heavy fabric, leaving the individual with a feeling of nakedness against the cold weather. The tires continue to roll over the asphalt road, hissing while spitting up the moisture behind them from the melted snow. Only the snow itself, piled up next to the road from days before, gives the visual contrast necessary to direct me through the streets to my destination on this gloomy day.

I firmly grip the wheel as I turn right onto Cherry St. The steering wheel is worn from what must have been several years of use. I suddenly feel it in my stomach now. The nervousness has slowly built up as I approach, but right at this moment, it really hits me. Perhaps a more substantial meal could have helped in tempering this feeling. I should have eaten something heavier this morning instead of the breakfast bars I frequently consume. If things do not go as well as planned, I may not be eating for a while. How could I have spent so much time and energy putting this together and forgot to plan on eating? I sure hope that overlooking a minor detail like this will not translate into exhibiting a more vital flaw missing from the plan.

The car heater, which took so long to take effect, is blasting heat like fire now. A slight burning smell from the vent accompanies this warmth. I hate these old vehicles. The heat takes forever to kick in, but when it eventually does, it spits directly into one's face bringing discomfort to the raw, vulnerable skin. The worst part is how it aggravates the eyes. The hot air blows onto the surface of the eyeball, making it dry, scratchy, and irritated.

I suddenly begin to fade from my surroundings, visualizing the job ahead of me. I walk through all the steps in my mind, following the execution of our plan and what we discussed to do in certain situations. If all goes well, it should be quick and painless with very little, if any, external complications. That is the thing about robberies, though. No matter how much you prepare and research, one wrong decision or sliver of bad luck can turn a perfect plan into a world of disaster. Plans will always have associated risks. Several variables are beyond our control in the development of a strategy. Some examples could be new security measures, police nearby, a Good Samaritan, or lack of cooperation with the employees and civilians inside. Even one of these factors could amplify the complexity of our operation.

This, being our first ever bank heist, will involve more risk than anything that we have done thus far. Most people do not think the risk is worth it. A typical small branch, such as the one we hope to break into, holds on average anywhere from $50,000 to $100,000 in the vault. This seems like a reasonable amount of money, but the penalty for being caught makes most people shy away from even considering it. Because the FDIC is an agency of the federal government, bank robberies are under federal jurisdiction involving the FBI. The mandated lengthy prison terms, enhanced by the carrying of loaded firearms, make criminals very wary of pulling off a job like this.

Of course, there are some crazy and impulsive crooks who attempt to rob from today's banks. They need money immediately to pay off a debt or to buy the drugs that control their lives. The associated risk does not enter the minds of these people. They live and act in the moment and do not think about the consequences of their actions. They have no definite plan and react to the situation that plays out. They are sloppy and uneducated in their execution and make an enormous mess of things. They are usually caught because of their stupidity.

I do not put myself in the same category as these people. We may all be grouped as criminals, which has a negative connotation in society, but I do not wish to be considered as one who does not comprehend the consequences of his own actions. I do indeed understand that I will go to jail for a long time if caught, and also know the physical and mental suffering inflicted upon others by the collateral damage of my actions.

You may be wondering why I choose to engage in criminal activity. Crime, itself, is an act forbidden by law and is liable for punishment. I have already mentioned that I understand the consequences. But crime is not necessarily morally wrong. Was selling alcohol during Prohibition morally wrong? Probably not. Many individuals may think that adhering to unlawful activity, in general, is morally wrong, and I commend their view, but I see "moral" as situational. In some criminal instances, it is easy to pinpoint the heinous decisions. I try not to follow sinful paths whenever it is deemed unnecessary. In some specific situations, these evil acts cannot be avoided and must be carried out for a job to be completed successfully.

Stealing for self-benefit and want, though, IS morally wrong. There is no way of getting around that fact, and there is no way in which I can make you think otherwise. But I want you to consider this: the act of stealing is so ingrained in human nature that it is sometimes hard to differentiate between what is right and wrong. Let me explain. As robbers and extortionists are associated with stealing, they are by no means the only people that make a living from it. The well-regarded businesses such as cell phone, credit card, cable, and other companies make their profits from charging everyday people with hidden fees and monetary punishments. People sue each other all the time over questionable matters, not because of the problems themselves, but for the chance to enrich themselves monetarily. Our society embraces this "taking from others" indirectly. The only reason I may be scorned and looked down upon in the public eye is that I am more open and direct in my attitude and behavior.

I take from others because I have no other job. I have tried to work for legitimate companies, but have found them all to provide very little excitement and satisfaction. I do not want to waste my days sitting at a desk while watching the hours of my life pass by. All of those jobs would have put food on the table, but I was not gratified doing them. A few close friends from my childhood shared these same views, and somewhere down the line, one of us proposed the idea of stealing for a living. I do not remember who originally introduced the concept, or how he even persuaded us in this endeavor, but we eventually embraced the idea and tried it out. We knocked over gas stations and small businesses, living off of the divided earnings from them. It was never an enormous amount of money we acquired, but reasonable gains that satisfied us.

It is hard to express the euphoria surrounding the work that we do. Unlike the tedious jobs that consume life at a desk, this profession produces thrills and ecstasy caused by the risk of each situation. The adrenaline courses through our veins as every moment feeds off of the next. Our pulse rates quicken with the heightened tension in the room. Every second fills with excitement due to the uncertainty of what is to unfold in the upcoming moments. The entirety of the situation is intense. Those that are not expecting such an exciting day become frantic the instant we appear on the scene. From the first time we experienced this delirium, we knew immediately that this is how we would make our living.

It is, of course, just a matter of time before we are caught and locked away. No group is lucky enough to continue to pull off robberies without slipping up somehow. It is in our best interest to keep suspicion and evidence to a minimum in an attempt to extend our reign of burglaries. One of the most vital aspects of preparing for a particular job is choosing a strategic location. Robberies should not take place within a certain radius of each other at a consistent frequency. Sooner or later, investigators or the businesses themselves will be able to predict the patterns of our heists and increase lookout or security measures. Trying to avoid this is a difficult task, so we had to plan the location "hits" carefully. We had to wait long stretches of time and even traveled across state lines before pulling off a job. We did this to minimize law enforcement suspicion and to prevent them from making the connections to our past heists. The four of us have yet to be branded a group name, like Butch Cassidy's Hole-in-the-Wall gang or the Dalton gang. Pretty soon, we will be linked to all of our past crimes and be given a name. Once that happens, we will be just about finished.

Two more exits until we reach the road to our destination. The trip, which would feel like an eternity to travel to on any other occasion, seems undesirably short right now. I have always felt this way on rides to a job. The reason must be that I cannot possibly review all the minute details about our mission in one car trip. My nervousness causes me to overthink and question what I am doing. I have gone through everything I need to know multiple times and understand what to do in any given situation. I am an expert. This thought quickly settles me down. Currently, I am in the best possible position and cannot be more prepared for the job ahead.

My good friends are more than reliable as well. I have spent most of my life alongside them, and I trust them wholeheartedly. They are just as experienced as I am and know all of the twists and turns of the execution process. We have been doing this together since the very beginning when the initial idea was conceived. All of us were childhood friends, having known each other from our youthful days of tee-ball. I know each of their mothers, although most of the time we would hang out at the Celetta house where Mrs. Celetta would sometimes make meals for us. Years have gone by, but our friendships have remained strong, if not gotten stronger.

I grab the ski mask sitting in the passenger seat and pull it over my head with my right hand while my left controls the wheel. It is better that I put the mask on now before we get too close. My gloves are already on. I never trust fingerprints because police can retrieve them from anywhere. I always put the gloves on before I leave the house, knowing that every surface from then on is safe from the oil residue that fingers leave behind. Also, had I not thought about putting them on earlier, police could easily connect me to this stolen vehicle.

Christmas Eve is the best time to pull off a bank robbery. The bank holds more cash than usual (the amount I mentioned earlier) due to all the transactions that take place on this day. We should be able to make more of a profit than we would on any other day because the bank does not like to hold onto a considerable sum of money for too long. Police response will be sluggish due to the large volume of last-minute shoppers on the roads. As long as there is not an officer in the area, we will have enough time to get in and out before any resistance arrives. That is why we specifically chose this relatively remote bank. It is far from the mall and other specialty shops.

There have been several bank robberies committed around Christmastime, or Christmas Eve in particular, but the one that keeps popping up in my head is that of the infamous Santa Claus bank robbery. This historic robbery took place in the town of Cisco, Texas on December 23, 1927, and involved four different robbers. One of these robbers, who would have been recognized from a prior heist in the area, disguised himself in a Santa Claus outfit. The suit concealed his identity sufficiently without suspicion, but while withdrawing the cash, a gunfight broke out with the police and civilians that gathered outside the building. It was a messy situation, but the robbers escaped, leading to the largest manhunt in the state. In the end, one of the four robbers died from gunshot injuries while bullet wounds injured the rest. Eight innocent others were wounded at the bank and during the chase that ensued. The remaining thieves were eventually caught, and two of the three were sentenced to death. Only one man was sentenced to life imprisonment, but he was paroled in the mid-1940s.

The events of this Santa Claus bank robbery stuck with me throughout this planning process, proving to me how real and dangerous a situation like robbing a bank can actually be. Only one made it out of the entire operation alive. This real danger is why I plan so hard and think about every controllable angle – things can quickly turn into chaos with only one tiny mishap.

I need to take this next exit. I glance at the side view mirror to make sure nobody is in the adjacent lane so I can move over. Ha! There he is. Fifty-or-so yards back is Marco in his red vehicle, already sporting a ski mask similar to mine. I cannot see, but I wonder if both Teddy and Sergio are directly behind him.

Marco and Sergio Celetta are brothers. Sergio is my age, and Marco just a year younger. As I mentioned earlier, when we were kids, we used to hang out at the Celetta's house. Their home had all the newest games, and we entertained ourselves there for years. I consider Sergio to be my best friend and right-hand man. I am sure he would say the same thing about me. Back in the early days, Sergio and I came up with ideas of things to do as a group, and we always supported each other. Theodore Lagutus, or "Teddy" to us, is four years my junior and has always been treated as a younger brother. We accepted him into our small group from the time we first met him, and he has remained loyal to us "older boys" ever since. We used to give Teddy so much hell back in those days, not out of hate, but because of the age difference and how easy it was to pull a funny prank on him. Teddy always stayed with us, though. As he grew older, he worked his way up to be our equal. Even though Teddy was a little sidekick to all of us, I felt that he would respect my decisions the most and stand by my side when needed. I trust each member of our group with my life and would not feel as secure about a job without them watching my back.

There it is! I see it in my view now. This is the bank where we will execute our heist. I see maybe a dozen cars in the parking lot, and there are no police vehicles in sight. This is going to be a go! My heart instantly starts racing. The instant surge of excitement hits my stomach hard and almost makes me want to vomit. As I pull into the lot, I experience the overwhelming physical urge to get started.

Sergio and Teddy are sitting in the lot as I pull in. I guess I was incorrect in thinking that they were behind Marco. They separated themselves a few spots in front of the building so that both vehicles would not be blocked in if law enforcement happened to park behind them. I park my car two rows behind them so that I can give them the signal when all is ready.

I quickly gather myself before taking any action. I give Marco a few seconds to get parked into a spot and prepare himself for what comes next. I have everything with me that I need. I glance at the time on the dashboard once more. Perfect! It is precisely the time we planned on getting here. I take a deep breath to help me relax and attempt to temper my emotions. No going back now.

I nod once to signify the go. In unison, all four of us open our doors and step out onto the wet pavement. Marco and I sprint over to Sergio and Teddy so that we can enter the building together. As I meet up with them, I catch a glimpse of Sergio's face. I cannot see his face behind the mask, but his wide brown eyes tell me that he is fearful about the job ahead of us. I find this odd. Sergio is usually the calm one when it comes to execution. The fact that this is a riskier job must be getting to him a little more than our previous heists. When we get close, Sergio puts his hand out to throw open the glass door in front of us.

"Here we go!!!" I yell as he violently thrusts the entrance door open and we all rush inside behind him.

CHAPTER 2

After breaching the entrance, all four of us immediately scatter toward our assigned positions in the building. The recently unsuspecting occupants of the bank become frozen from this sudden frenzy, not initially out of fear, but from being caught off-guard and forced into the real world from their holiday fantasies. Each of us begins wielding our weapons. I whip out my pistol, brandishing my weapon to send the message that I am not here to joke around. A woman screams from the left side of the building. Panic and horror follow the scream as the atmosphere becomes drenched with dread.

"Get the Fuck on the ground!" Sergio howls, waving his gun to emphasize the urgency.

"Except you," he waves at those behind the counter. "You tellers stand tall and step back against the wall. I don't want any movement or action on your part. If all of you listen to me and everything goes smoothly, you will all make it home safely for the holidays."

Both Sergio and Teddy hop over the teller's counter to secure the rear of the bank. They disappear together into the back room, leaving Marco and me to take care of the front. Marco darts behind the counter to begin collecting all of the cash from each of the teller stations. To not make a mess of things, or more importantly, to not destroy all the money from the potential dye packs, Marco places each stack into a different Ziploc bag. We are willing to allow one of the stacks of bills to be ruined as long as the rest are fine. We will only be able to make out with a few thousand dollars up front here, so Sergio and Teddy need to open the safe in the back for us to make any real profit. They will need to work in a hurry because a silent alarm was probably already set, and if not, Marco surely will set one off soon by pulling a wrong stack of bills. That is why the locked safe needs to be opened as quickly as possible. To open the safe, we will need the combination that only the acting bank manager will know. Any other person working today will not know it or be of any help to us. Finding the bank manager is my responsibility. Now it is time for me to put on a violent and frantic performance.

"Where is the bank manager?" I demand to the crowd.

I give it a few moments, but nobody answers. I walk around the front of the room to make sure everyone sees me. Six tellers stand behind the counter. This bank would typically have only three or four tellers at work, but they scheduled a few more employees today to meet the anticipated increase in traffic flow. I then count the number of customers lying on the floor. There are an even ten, three males and seven females. As I step by each terrified individual, I can hear their heavy breathing. I walk by a man crouched on the floor wearing a navy parka. I overhear him whispering prayers to himself. Some people seem less afraid than others. They must not perceive a true sense of urgency in our demands or demeanor. I need to make them feel differently.

"I'll ask once more," I state clearly. "Where is the manager?"

Nothing.

Time is ticking. I scan the room for any visual hints of who this manager might be. This is no help. I need to act instead of wasting more time.

"Do you people think this is a joke?"

I turn to the tellers behind the counter. I direct my attention to the last one on the left, a young girl with curly blonde hair. She is standing tall against the wall as Sergio demanded, but is quivering uncontrollably from fear.

"Excuse me, Miss, do you know who the manager is here?"

"I do," she answers and begins to sob. "I....don't...... know where...he....is right now, though."

This cute, innocent, young girl in her uniform black vest must have never been put into a situation even remotely similar to this. Despite her training and understanding of what to do if faced with a robber, she cannot handle the realistic pressure of it.

A quick idea passes through my head. I brush it away at first due to the nature of the thought, but as I consider it again, it seems like a viable option. Time is of the essence right now.

"I'll tell you what then," I turn around in a circle and shout so that a hiding manager can hear me. "I'm a busy man and don't have the time to put up with this shit, so I'm gonna give you, the manager of this place, five seconds to show yourself before I end this young lady's life."

"NO! NO! NO!" The woman suddenly bawls as I direct the gun toward her forehead. "PLEASE!...NO!... Please don't do this to me!"

I have no intention to kill the poor girl but must do something this drastic to get the guy to show himself. The manager's lack of cooperation will not be the reason we fail. We have worked too long and hard to give up because of this.

"Show yourself!" I roar. "Five!"

13

The woman's sobbing continues as she keeps begging for her life.

"Four!"

I have killed before, but only out of necessity. Sergio, Marco, and Teddy cannot and have not killed before and probably would not be able to do it. Therefore, I am the only one who can carry out a stunt like this.

"Three!"

With all the criminal acts the three have committed, they will not accept the act of killing as a means to get things accomplished. They may act tough and violent, but it is all a show. Acting tough and violent is one thing, but sending a clear message will immediately invoke cooperation.

"Two!"

I, too, hate this action, but it must be done. It has to. The fear of a threat is only useful if it is believable.

Why is this guy not showing himself? I am begging on the inside. PLEASE SHOW YOURSELF.

"One!"

Both the woman and I cannot believe it. I stare into her beautiful blue eyes. The tears that stream across her face are real. I feel both them and her pain. Her life should not be taken. It should not be cut short because of me in what should be such a happy time of year. Goodbye, I tell her without opening my mouth. I pull the trigger.

Her body becomes lifeless as it falls to the floor. The tears on her face have stopped, but now the streams of fiery blood run in their place. The shell of the young beauty collapses to the hard bank floor.

Following the initial shock of my action, I close my eyes for a few seconds to dispel as much emotion and distress as possible. My right hand, which still holds the sinful weapon, begins trembling violently. I suppress my shaking hand by holding it tightly to my side so that nobody can see the vulnerability I possess after taking a life. I take a deep breath to regain composure.

Everything is so quiet. After all of the crying and yelling and screaming, the room is nothing but silent. If it were not for the post-gunshot ringing in our ears, you could hear a pin drop. I can feel the quiet judgment around me, from all the civilians and probably even my friends. Without looking around the room, I can sense everyone's eyes on me. I feel naked and dirty. I am exposed.

I glance over at Marco at the other end of the counter. He has ceased collecting the money and stares at me. He is lost in thought trying to understand what just took place.

I need to push these thoughts out of my head. I can think about this later, but now I have to get back to work.

"Okay," I finally speak to the crowd. They continue to fight back their tears and restrain trembling at the sound of my voice. "You can see from this demonstration that I mean what I say. I am not afraid to act on my demands and will kill again. Until the manager shows himself, I will keep taking lives."

One woman screams after hearing these words. The room again fills with the sounds of sobbing and muffled prayers. They would give or do anything in their power to return safely to their toasty homes and beautiful families.

"Please! Please! Pleeaase!" cries an unfamiliar man I hear running from the back.

His distressed pleas surprise me, and I whip my body around with my pistol extended to see who is approaching. The man, seeing my weapon directed at him, immediately halts and throws his hands up.

"Don't Shoot! Don't Shoooot!"

The gentleman is somewhat pudgy, balding, and looks to be middle-aged. I watch as the water pools in the lower parts of his eyes and causes tears to run wildly down until they hang at the bottom of his chin. He looks down at the body of the gunned victim. He drops his right arm to wipe the tears on his shirtsleeve.

"I cannot believe I did this," he laments as he raises his eyes to me. "I am the manager."

I just look at him. He is a defeated man and will forever be ashamed and feel guilty about the event that has happened here today. He will not forgive himself and will never live it down. It will be a burden he carries to his grave.

Teddy emerges from the back of the bank and grasps this man by his arm, yanking him back to the vault room. The man surrenders himself with his head down while following Teddy so that we can finish our job. Both the manager and Teddy disappear into the back room to work on the safe with Sergio. As long as the time lock to the safe is not set (we know it should not be due to our prior research), Sergio and Teddy will be able to enter it with the manager's combination.

How did the manager elude both Sergio and Teddy as they cleared the back room with the safe? He must have had a pretty good hiding place. I peer around the corner and see a small closet with the door ajar in the short hallway that separates the front and back of the building. Upon this discovery, I shake my head and get back to the current situation.

"We shouldn't be here too much longer," I say to everyone. "If you sit tight as we finish up, you will all be able to make it back home to see your loved ones soon. Don't mess it up and try anything stupid, though, or I will make sure that you don't make it out of here."

I step behind the counter to help Marco finish getting all the bills from the register into individual Ziploc bags. In the development of our plan, we discussed that I should not help with the bagging of the money. I was supposed to watch over the civilians and only take action if needed. I would stick to this plan in any other case, but I feel I should clear the register of the fallen blonde girl. I do not want Marco to have to work over a corpse that may elicit any more emotion to his already stressed condition. I did this dirty deed, so I should be the one to face the graphic scene.

The people in the bank will not pose a problem as we finish up, but I will still keep a close watch while emptying the register. I glance down and see a pool of scarlet blood that covers a significant portion of the floor around her. I grab a few plastic bags from Marco and soil my boots in the gore surrounding the lifeless body.

"We're in!" I hear Sergio shout from the other part of the building.

Nice. It appears that retrieving the money will be successful. After securing the cash in the vault, the only problems to anticipate are any complications with our departure. The getaway itself is not the only worry in our escape, but the minimization of any clues or leads that could potentially steer investigators to us is also of vital importance.

Collecting the money from this register is not too much of a task. Marco has already finished retrieving all of the bills from the others and is impatiently waiting at the other end of the counter. He keeps his eyes focused on the front of the building and the customers sprawled out on the floor, but I do see him catch a glimpse of the body under me. Although he does not want to look at such a gruesome sight, his curiosity gets the better of him.

I try to shake the image of the scene below me as I shove the last couple of stacks into separate plastic bags. I concentrate on the current situation to keep my mind off of it. Other than the short delay in finding the manager, everything seems to be going fairly routinely. Nothing has come up yet that has been a severe snag in carrying this out or extended the amount of time we plan to spend in here. Sergio and Teddy will be ready soon, and we will be on our way.

Marco walks over to me to collect the stacks that I put in the plastic bags. I slide them along the counter so that he does not have to drench his shoes in the bloody puddle underneath me. He promptly pulls them into the bag where he placed all the other Ziplocs. He then returns to the other end of the counter.

"Okay," Marco says. "All of you working here behind the counter need to make your way to the front of the building." He gestures in front of him, "I want you to sit with the customers in the lobby."

One by one, the employees move from behind the counter to the front. We planned this so that when it came time to escape, all of the customers and employees would be in the same place so we could keep an eye on them.

Almost no time passes before Sergio emerges out from the back room carrying a pack that he and Teddy filled with the vault's capital. Standing only feet away in the front of the hallway, he glances over at me and then in the direction of Marco.

"You alright and good to go? Let's get out of here," he says.

Marco nods then lunges toward the front exit.

"Wait! Wait! Wait! We all need to leave together. Wait for him!" I call to Marco, referring to Teddy. "What is taking him so long?"

"I don't know, he should've been all finished packin' up with me," Sergio replies as he moves to face me. "Hey! Get your ass out front here. We need to move it, Pronto!"

I look toward the doors out front where Marco waits and is antsy to get going.

"Stay here and watch," I direct Sergio as I try to push to get by him. "I'm gonna check to see what's taking him so long."

18

As I pass by him, I feel Sergio's hand clench around my wrist.

"I'm so sorry that I have to do this. This must be done."

At hearing these words from Sergio's mouth, I instantly become confused. I whip around to question that statement asking "Wha…?"

I cannot finish the question, as I am cut off by the butt of Sergio's gun crashing down onto my head. All goes black.

The Bad Guy

CHAPTER 3

The incident happened a long time ago. I was about twelve years old when we had our first experience of group conflict. I cannot remember another event that could have ended our relationship more than the one that occurred on this particular day. Had we not been so forgiving of each other, this episode could have divided our circle of friends. We would not have discovered the rush of excitement in committing robberies or the fulfillment in carrying them out if we did not decide to stay together. It is interesting to look back and see how much everything could have changed if we had actually split up. Maybe, just maybe, I would not have caused all the devastation that keeps me up at night.

We were not a perfect group of four. No group ever is. I imagine that all friendships have seen their share of drama, conflict, or social dilemma. That is why friends drift away from each other over time. There are differences of opinions. People change, have different mindsets or goals, and leave those confidants to pursue their own aspirations. They find new groups or new companions to better suit them for the ambitions they hope to achieve.

The four of us did not need to change our mindset – our goals were one. Though conflict came and left, in the end, we melded our hopes and wishes, and all benefited from it. We were happy, that is, most of the time. Our differences were not enough to split us apart. The strength of our bond has been the one thing that allows us to live every day without fear, knowing that someone has your back at all times. Many friendships have broken apart at some point, but ours has stayed stable over the years. I would not have enough courage to go through with these heists without knowing that the other three were right behind me.

Even with this mindset, there is always that ounce of uncertainty. No one readily accepts another person's ideas without some sort of scrutiny. I also question my views on occasion and ask myself if this is what I really want. At the end of the day, I still trust myself and my friends. I do not want to believe that the individuals behind me are only looking out for themselves.

Perhaps I am overthinking this. Intentions can be misunderstood. It is not always black and white when it comes to determining what is best for everyone. Depending on the situation, a well-intentioned decision can subtly leave a lasting adverse impact.

As much as I want to believe in this, a few incidents from the past bring these beliefs and trusts into question. Why do I remember these events so vividly unless they mean something?

All of us were walking back to the Celetta household after buying some ice cream from Ernie's small shop down the street. The sun vigorously beat down on this mid-summer day. We walked by the line of well-kept suburban houses, each one surrounded by their lush, freshly-cut green grass lawns. The sun blazed at its highest point of the day, not tainting the ground with shadows that would cover up any detail of the beautiful neighborhood landscape.

Nobody was out and about on such a bright day due to the harsh summer heat. Imagine opening an oven to withdraw some cookies. All that concentrated heat surrounds your face and arms, making it almost unbearable as your eyes water to adjust. Now think about how that would feel wrapped around your entire body. It was not one of the better days to enjoy the summer weather.

The ice cream itself was the only reason why such a climate could be tolerable. The cold, creamy, vanilla remedy tasted better than it would on an average day. It needed to be ingested quickly, though, as the sun caused it to melt at such a rapid rate. If you did not lick a particular side of it at the right time, the melted cream would dribble down the cone and sticky-up your fingers. Staying clean while eating the ice cream became an art.

We all laughed at young eight-year-old Teddy as he had trouble doing this. His hands were drenched in vanilla soup as it ran down his elbows, his shirt was wet in places where it dripped onto it, and his pudgy face showed signs of white where it missed his mouth. Teddy did not say a word and was happy as he concentrated on finishing his cone.

"Check out Teddy!" Marco chuckled. "Are you trying to eat it or take a bath in it?"

We continued laughing at his remark. Even Teddy giggled at his own sloppiness.

"I don't blame him." Sergio calmed himself down and said, "I'm having enough trouble myself trying to get it before it melts."

"Wooo! It sure is a hot one!" I remarked.

"Yeah," he returned, "I don't even want to be out here anymore."

"I need to go inside!" Teddy blurted.

"Don't worry, little bud," I assured. "We'll be home pretty soon."

I turned around to the group. "Do you guys want to go back and watch some T.V.?"

"Yeah, we can do that," Marco said. "Teddy's favorite show is probably on right now."

Sergio was confused. "What show is that?"

Marco quickly answered, "*Are You Afraid of the Dark?*"

Teddy immediately responded, "No! No! No! I do not like that one. It is way *way* too scary!"

We all burst into laughter again.

"Good ol' Teddy," I said as I patted his back.

"You sure are funny," Sergio confirmed.

We continued walking down the street in the quiet neighborhood. Had it not been for the heat, it could have been a relaxing day. You could sit out, perhaps read a book, chat with a friend, enjoy the soothing sounds of nature, or smell the fresh grass and the scent of the trees. For us at that age, a fun game of wiffle ball would have sufficed. Instead of walking for ice cream, we could have pulled a game together and avoided what happened next.

We were not far from the Celetta's house when we ran into them. I saw them in the distance but did not recognize who they were at first. As we got closer, I identified the smaller one. It was Crevan Sneckle. Crevan was a lot younger than me but was an evil little boy. Everything about this kid was foul. He wore a tight smirk on his face that, contrasted with his sharp dark eyes, gave the visual evidence of someone up to no good. He lacked respect for anyone around him and would look for any possible way to cause trouble. He was a juvenile who would throw rocks at random house windows, scrape the paint off of cars parked in the street, and intimidate kids around his age for his own amusement. Even the name itself, Crevan Sneckle, gave the impression of wickedness.

The other boy was his brother, Coy. Coy was a year older than Sergio and me and could not maintain control of his younger brother. Their mother made him watch Crevan, even though it was an impossible task to ask of anyone. Coy lived up to the definition of his name and was a quiet and shy individual who basically followed Crevan around. I felt sorry for the kid. He was not happy with the job assigned to him and was uncomfortable with this designated duty.

As they got closer, the feeling of impending trouble heightened within me. If we could just walk by with little interaction or notice, we could get home without any conflict. My concern intensified with every step that drew us nearer. I looked over at Sergio and Marco and saw that they had prepared themselves as I had, hoping for no interaction as well. The tension was obvious to everyone but Teddy. He did not even notice Crevan and Coy approaching but was looking down upon his ice cream, determined to finish the soupy mess.

Crevan spoke, just as I knew he would. "What's up, boys?"

"Nothing," Sergio said, in an attempt to end the conversation quickly. "We just got some ice cream and are now going home to watch some television."

"Television?" Crevan got a strange look on his face. "Are you serious? Who the hell calls it that? Real people just say T.V."

"We don't want to cause any trouble," I said. "Let us go home, and you can do whatever you were going to do."

"Dontcha wanna know what *we're* doing out here?" Crevan asked. "Like a good person, I asked you. Don't you have the same respect as that?"

"Let's just keep going," Coy attempted to persuade Crevan. "Let's not waste any time and keep moving."

Crevan turned around. "Shut up, Coy! I don't care what you have to say."

I directed our group from the confrontation. "Just keep on walking and ignore him. We don't need to talk."

As I directed, Sergio, Marco, and Teddy continued silently. We started walking past the two brothers and gave them the cold shoulder.

"You think you're all some sort of hotshots?" Crevan yelled, obviously getting frustrated. "Think you are all way too cool to talk to me? Bunch of bitches!"

We kept moving, taking the abuse from the infuriated, rotten-mouthed little kid. His face had begun to turn red with a vein pulsating out from the inflamed forehead. It was not in his nature to let this go. His impulse was to act, to be heard, to catch our attention in some way. As Crevan passed by, he must have looked over at the ice cream-eating Teddy. This innocent young boy would be Crevan's next victim.

Teddy, who was too preoccupied to listen to what Crevan was saying, and unaware of his surroundings in general, kept his goal on the dessert in hand. As soon as Crevan passed him, he swatted down upon Teddy's forearm, knocking the runny ice cream cone from his hands onto the ground. It splattered all across the pavement.

"There!" Crevan shouted. "Why dontchu eat that shit off the ground then?"

Teddy stood there, puzzled for a moment. He gazed downward at the creamy mess and watched as the liquid flowed into one of the creases on the sidewalk. His eyes then rose from the street to look at Crevan. Teddy's expression was that of mortification. He looked helpless, a child forced into a situation. He was minding his own business and was involuntarily put on the spot.

"Whatcha gon' do about it?" Crevan egged on Teddy. "You wanna hit me?"

I stepped in. "Teddy, let's go back to my house. If you still want some, we have some ice cream in the freezer there."

"No dude," Sergio disagreed. "He needs to stand up for himself. Let him fight 'em. Go on, Teddy, teach his ass a lesson!"

Teddy stood there, looking uncomfortable. He was not a fighter. He was just a calm, little boy who did not bother anyone and shied away from conflict. Even if he were to fight Crevan, he would not be able to hurt him. Crevan picked fights all the time, and though they were about the same age and stature, there was no comparison. Crevan was an experienced and dirty fighter and Teddy was merely a peacekeeper. It is not in Teddy's nature to resort to violence.

Marco jumped by his brother's side. "Come on, lil' Ted! Throw a punch! It is your time to shine!"

"Do this for yourself!" Sergio added. "He won't mess with you ever again after this."

"No, Teddy!" I interrupted. "I've got to look out for you. You can't win this fight. Let's just get out of here."

"Come on, man," Sergio addressed me this time. "He needs this. If he runs away from this fight, he is going to run away from them for the rest of his life. He needs to face things at some point. That day needs to be today."

"That's not true," I said. "We look out for each other, and I'm not going to allow him to do this. This isn't a fight. He is just going to get himself hurt."

"What are ya, some kind of pussy?" Crevan continued to provoke.

"Yeah, come on, Kev," Marco joined in. "He needs this. This could be a breakout moment for him."

Teddy scrunched up his face, looking uneasy. "I can't do it. No, no, no. I just can't."

"Yeah you can, bud," Sergio encouraged. "Just do it. We all have your back."

I argued, "No, Ted. Just come with me. I am here for you, and *I* always have your back. Walk away from this one."

A tear came to Teddy's eye and ran down his soft cheek. Teddy was torn between us in the group and did not know what to do. He was going to listen to me, though, as he respected my decision the most.

"Aw, poor baby, gonna cry?" Crevan continued as he brought a fist to his own eye to rub the fake tears from it. "Boo-hoo."

"Don't cry, man," Sergio smiled toward Teddy. "You got this. This guy ain't nothin'."

"I'm sorry!" Teddy blurted as tears now flowed from his face.

He sniffled and suddenly sprinted down the sidewalk toward his home. I heard him gasp for breaths of air in between his cries.

"Wait up, buddy!" I yelled after him as he took off down the street.

"Haha! What a wimp," Crevan scorned. "He probably did the smart thing, though, knowing that I was gonna kick his ass."

"Shut up!" I said, turning my attention from Teddy to face Crevan.

"Don't tell me that! You wanna start something now? You don't want this little boy to beatchu up, huh?"

After all the snide remarks we took from Crevan, in addition to holding back from engaging in any confrontation, my fuse quickly ran out. I was not going to take it from this little kid. He ruined such a pleasant summer day for us, and I would not endure any more abuse. I was fuming with rage, a wave of anger that immediately pulsed through my system.

"I don't *care* how old you are! I don't care about you! You tried to hurt my little man, and now I am going to hurt you!"

I dove at him. Crevan's expression shot from one of pure satisfaction to that of terror in a split second. I flung my fists into that terrible little visage of his as hard and as fast as I could.

"Ow! No! Please stop!" he screamed as I poured my hatred into his disgusting face.

It took some time before Sergio, Marco, and Coy could wrestle me off of Crevan. They pulled me away from him, and my aggression eventually subsided.

"Calm down, calm down," Marco repeated.

"Let's get out of here," Coy yelled as he tugged the willing Crevan away from us.

They hurried down the street together. Crevan did not say a word as they ran off. He followed Coy while holding his beaten and bloodied face.

"What was that for?!" Sergio lectured as both he and Marco held onto me.

"Get off of me!" I shouted. "What do you mean 'what was that for?!'"

"You went off on that little kid," Sergio replied.

"I was teaching his ass a lesson. Isn't that what you told Teddy to do?"

"That was different," Marco jumped in.

"I am pissed," I said. "What were you trying to do to Teddy?"

"Nothin' man," Sergio said. "I just thought it would be cool to see Teddy get into it a little bit. You know, fight on his own for once."

I whipped my body around to loosen my arms from Sergio's and Marco's grasp.

"That's not right!" I screamed at them as I broke free.

"Come on, man! Just cool off," cried Marco.

I caught my breath before speaking. "We've got to look out for Teddy. He is our friend, and we can't let people like Crevan mess with him. Crevan would've hurt him, you know that. It wouldn't have been a fight at all. We would've had to jump in right away to stop it. We should've avoided the matter entirely. I told you that we just needed to walk away, but you didn't listen. You guys are just too stupid. Teddy ran off crying anyway. Do you guys even care about how he feels?"

"Sure we do," Marco said. "He is our little man."

"No, you don't understand," I said. "He is just a little person you all pick on. I'm the only one who actually cares about how he thinks and feels. You all just make fun of him and keep him around for entertainment."

"You know that isn't true," Sergio responded. "Just think about it. We are all tight. Why would we let him hang out all the time if we didn't care about him?"

"That doesn't make any sense," I said. "Enjoying Teddy being around isn't the same as caring about him."

With that last statement, Sergio looked to be rubbed the wrong way. Sergio does not appreciate having to explain his actions or defend himself. My scrutiny was not going to be taken lightly. His anger kept building as I continued discussing his and Marco's apparent lack of affection toward Teddy. He clenched his teeth and was done being defensive.

"Seriously dude," Sergio said with some hostility. "I care for him. How dare you question my friendship! I'm just trying to help!"

I was not going to back down this time either. I did not care how good of a friend Sergio was to me. He was going to face the hard facts and accept the anxiety that he caused Teddy and me just moments ago.

"Why don't you go chase Teddy down right now like a good friend should?" I said. "Tell him that you really are sorry!"

Sergio was way too full of himself to take something like that from me. It did not matter if what I told him to do was right or not. He does not take kindly to commands no matter how justified they are, not even from me.

"You should go since you love him so much!" he yelled. "Maybe then you can give him a little kiss too!"

I yelled back as I raised my fists, "Screw you! How about you kiss these?"

"You know who you sound like right now?" Marco jumped in at me.

I did not care what Marco had to say, but I answered him anyway. "No, who?"

"You sound just like Crevan Sneckle trying to pick a fight! The guy you hate so much! You are just like him right now!"

"Yeah, you are!" Sergio agreed with his brother. "And maybe I'll have to act like you, Kevin, go crazy and beat you up."

"Shut up, guys!" I exclaimed. "You just back each other up because you're brothers. I am nothing like Crevan, you know that. I actually care about people."

"Whatever," Sergio said. "If you had the opportunity to take advantage of someone, you'd do it."

"Never!" I said. "Screw you! I was not the one who hung a friend out to dry today."

I was livid. I did not even want to argue with them anymore. They were so wrong. They were so wrong about everything.

"I'm going to see how Teddy is doing as a good friend should do."

With that, I was done arguing with them. I turned around and started running down the street in the direction of Teddy's house, leaving both Sergio and Marco in my dust. I was not going to give them a chance to say anything back to me.

As I began to run, I shouted one more thing at them. I was so positive about it at the time, something I knew was so entirely true. I yelled, "I don't want to be your friend anymore!"

CHAPTER 4

I wake up and my head throbs. My forehead pulsates violently from the blood flooding to swell the raw wound. On top of the swelling, I begin to battle a pounding headache that increases its intensity in correlation with my growing awareness.

After my body registers the initial pain, my mind attempts to recall the events that recently transpired and brought me to this point. I visualize Sergio standing there and bringing the handle of his weapon down across the left side of my head that now throbs. What was he doing? Lying on the ground confused, I ask myself an even better question: What exactly has happened since then?

I suddenly feel a cold wetness across the left part of my face. The ski mask is still on my head but is entirely drenched in some sort of liquid. Perhaps Sergio's pistol created a deep laceration that allowed such an injury to discharge so quickly. The mask is too soaked for only sweat to have caused this. I force my eyes open to better comprehend where I am and figure out why my visage is sodden with this fluid.

My vision is a blur. The moment my eyelids slide apart, all I see is a dark crimson sea. My eyesight slowly clears, and I become shocked at what I see. My stomach clenches at the horror of such a sight. The deceased blonde cashier lies next to me, a few feet away. Her face gazes right back at me. Her blue eyes stay open, staring into mine, into the killer who deserves to be the dead one lying here. Above those piercing eyes is the hole in her forehead that gives way to the stream of blood that creeps its way across the contrasting white tile floor. My crown lies right in the middle of this puddle of her blood. The black mask I wear is saturated with it. I gag at this realization. I would puke, but because of all the energy my body is expending from the pain in my throbbing head, I cannot force myself to do it.

I vigorously attempt to put this sickening picture out of my mind and try to ignore the pounding in my head as I quickly evaluate the current situation. I am still here in the bank, so I must not have been unconscious for too long. How long have I been out? This question is of vital importance. If it has been within a minute or two, I still have a chance to get up and escape without police intervention. If not, though, they may already be here on the premises. If I get up right now, I can either make the quick escape or immediately be cuffed and thrown in the back of their vehicle. I wish I had not been knocked out behind the counter so I can see what is going on. My decision needs to be made now before it is too late. I will get up and go because there is at least a slight chance for an escape.

I start doing a push-up to lift myself from the ground. I am glad that I am wearing gloves so I do not have to feel the fluids between my fingers.

I hear the front door smack open and the sound of footsteps rushing in. "Are there any more of them in here?" shouts a deep male voice.

Damn! They are already here. I relax my arms from pushing myself up as I settle back down into the gore. There goes the idea of getting up and escaping. I will continue to lie here and act unconscious. I will see how far this gets me.

"There's one behind the counter!" a different man's voice quickly responds. "He has a gun, and he shot the teller!"

I lie immobile and squint my eyes so I can still see, but keep them closed enough to give the impression of being unconscious. Since we moved the employees out from behind the counter earlier, no one saw me move and will still believe I am passed out. It is hard to suppress the pumping of my nervous heart. The policeman is going to see me any second now. I cannot mess this up. What is he going to do when he sees me? What am I going to do?

I hear him take a quick breath above me, probably from the unexpected sight of blood surrounding us. "What a mess," he says softly to himself.

"Is this his blood, her blood, or both?" he asks.

"I don't know," the other male responds. "He never got shot, but he took a hell of a blow to the head by his one of his buddies."

"Well, he sure is breathing heavily," the cop says. "Rick! Rick! Get over here! I've got another one! He is knocked out, but still alive."

The cop overhead, who called for Rick, starts making his way around the counter. Through my squinted eyes, I can see his weapon directed at me the entire way as he turns. He gingerly steps over the girl and carefully avoids getting blood on his shoes. I can barely see but can make out that his unarmed hand starts to grab the handcuffs by his belt.

Out from my confusion, aching head, and raw emotion, I feel a quick jolt of anger. This instantaneous anger courses through my body. Why am I the one here on the ground? Why have I been betrayed? Who decided that I should go to jail?

In the time it took for the cop to reach my motionless body, I made my decision. My years will not be wasted in some prison. I have pushed too far and given too much to yield myself powerless and surrender. I have always accepted the consequences surrounding my criminal actions and the high anticipation of being caught, but never under such a situation as this: by being stabbed in the back by those closest to me. This is not the time to call it quits. Now is the time for vengeance and to reclaim what they took from me. I may end up incarcerated one day, but that day is not today. I am going to leave this bank free and on my own or will be escorted out in a body bag. The death I am risking by undertaking this danger is not of importance. I would rather die here and now than spend my days dwindling away behind bars knowing that I have been wronged and cannot do anything about it.

In my peripherals, I notice the dropped weapon I held earlier lying in the red puddle only about two feet away from my head. The policeman lowers his body, pistol still outstretched, to reach and sling the cuffs around my right hand. The time to act is now.

CHAPTER 5

In one motion, I throw my body onto my left side and thrust a violent swing upward with my right arm to swat away the pistol directed at me. *BANG!* His gun discharges into the back wall. One woman screams from the sudden resurgence of hysteria. I slide my body across the wet floor and push my hand back down to grasp the butt of my weapon. After securing the gun in my hand, I hastily twist to face the policeman who is repositioning his aim. I dive for him as he pulls the trigger once more. *BANG!* I feel nothing as my shoulder collides into his chest. The bullet must have whizzed directly under my left arm. Following the blow to his sternum, I furiously begin smashing my pistol into his face while wrestling the weapon from his hand until he drops it. As I hear the sound of his firearm clunk against the floor, I promptly swing my body around him and press the barrel of my gun under his right ear. I tightly clench his collar and pull it toward me with my left hand. I finally catch a breath as I settle behind my new captive. I now have a hostage, a bargaining chip that I can hopefully use to get me out of this mess.

The events of the last few moments take everyone by surprise. The civilians in the bank become rattled again, realizing that the excitement of the day is not quite over yet. The other cop in the building, who was called earlier by the name Rick, must not have had the time to rush over to help out his partner. I take a look at my prisoner's face. Beyond the combination of bruises and blood, he gives a look of befuddlement, a look showing that he still cannot grasp the reality of what just happened. As I watch, I can see the physical changes taking place due to the swelling, especially in the lower lip that makes him look like he is pouting. He is too overwhelmed by the situation to have fear, so he just stares on ahead in astonishment.

"Hey, Rick!" I yell to signal his partner's attention.

"Yeah?" I hear him reply from behind the other side of the counter.

Rick was not able to get over in enough time to help out his buddy, and when things immediately started to quiet down, he must have stopped and knelt behind the counter. He must have sat there and contemplated the situation instead of popping up and potentially making matters worse. He probably thought that if he did show himself, either he or his partner, as a result of my fast-paced action, could have ended up with a bullet between the eyes.

"I have your friend," I continue to Rick. "I don't want to hurt him, but I'm not afraid to kill him if I need to. Don't do anything that could put his blood on your hands."

"Okay, Okay," he assures. "I don't want anything to happen either. What do you want?"

I tug on the prisoner's shirt and move my head close to whisper in his ear. "Get up slowly and don't try anything. I *Will* kill you. Just look at that girl on the floor."

I initiate our rise with a soft nudge from my pistol on his neck. We both slowly ascend together as I maintain a tight grasp on him and keep my weapon steadily pressed to the back of his head.

"Get away from the counter!" I demand to Rick.

He stands up and studies me carefully as he calmly steps back. He decides that there is no use in complicating this situation further, so he lets his weapon hang loosely at his side. He wants no conflict.

Now that I am in the favored position, I reply to Rick's unanswered question. "All I want is to get out of here as fast and as painlessly as possible."

He nods at my answer. I have the upper hand now. A little bit of excitement surges through me as I realize that escape is now an actual possibility. Rick is not going to make an aggressive move. The way he reacted to my scuffle with his partner is proof that he will not pose a problem.

Shit! My relief suddenly dissolves when I look out the front window. I see a vehicle in the distance with its blue and red lights swirling overhead and the irritating whine it makes as it darts in our direction.

I can deal with this. It is only another hurdle within this whole predicament. If I continue to focus and make the right decisions, I will still be able to leave. I just need to keep moving.

The vehicle circles around the parking lot and pulls up parallel to the building. It stops behind the first police car that arrived.

"Rick," I say. "It looks as though some more of your friends are here to interfere a bit."

Two officers leap out of the car and quickly settle themselves in a comfortable position behind it. Each one points his firearm toward the entrance.

"Here's the deal," I instruct Rick. "I want you to persuade them to come inside. Let them know that all I want is to escape and that nobody needs to get hurt. Don't fuck this up for me, though, or I may just shoot you."

He nods at my demand and swiftly makes his way to the door.

"Hey! One more thing."

He turns and directs his attention to me again.

"Make sure they know just how desperate and trigger-happy I am."

As I say these words, I drop my weapon to my side for a moment and fire a quick shot into the ground. *BANG!*

As I fire the weapon, everyone in the building instantly jumps. Rick does not think twice and hurriedly makes his way to the entrance door. The people on the floor suddenly become animated again, crying and praying. Each one of their bodies rises and falls due to increased heartbeats and rapid breathing. In a way, it is comical how the sound of a gun discharging can make a person react, especially when it is not expected. The noise is so incredibly loud that it interrupts any train of thought passing through the brain, and in their case, replaces the initial feeling of worry and insecurity into an instant moment of terror.

I gave Rick the task of bringing the two officers inside because if I can get everyone in the same area, it will produce fewer angles for anyone to take a shot at me from behind my hostage. I will be able to round the room and make it outside to a vehicle, having my hostage face all three policemen at the same time. That is part of the reason why I let Rick hold onto his gun and not set it on the floor. I would rather the indecisive Rick have it and be huddled together with the other two cops as I round the room. Additionally, I do not want a situation where a brave civilian makes a run for the gun and picks it up off the ground. I also keep a mental note that my hostage's gun is on the floor next to me. Nobody can see it behind the counter, so it is not a big deal that I leave it there.

I peer out the window and watch as the officers discuss their options. The one standing closest to the hood of the second police vehicle does not look very willing to react to my demands. Although I cannot understand his words as he talks to Rick, the dubious look on his face represents someone reluctant to agree right away. While studying his reactions, something peculiar catches my eye. I see something beyond Rick's body. No, that something is actually somebody. There is someone in the backseat of the first police vehicle that arrived.

I can only see part of the body because Rick is in my line of sight. My mind starts to race. Who is it? Did Sergio make it out? If it is him, I will make sure that son of a bitch gets a good view of my escape. Oh no, I think. It cannot be him. It is probably Teddy. I bet Sergio also knocked Teddy out while they were in the vault together. That is why I never saw Teddy come out from the back after the collection was complete. Sergio turned on Teddy and me and escaped with his brother. It is more profitable to split the bank cash-out two ways instead of our usual four. They must have decided to keep the money within their family. Their side plan was to stab both Teddy and me in the back. Those greedy bastards.

I look around the parking lot to make sure. Yes, I am correct. Both Teddy's and my stolen vehicles are still parked in the lot. Sergio's and Marco's are long gone. They escaped or at least got off the premises in their cars.

My present circumstance is the highest priority right now, though. I shift my gaze from the consultation outside to view the inside layout. If I were to move around the building, there is one threatening detail that could derail my wish for escape. People are scattered all along the bank floor. If I were to move across the room and skirt over the wrong good-willed individual, he could grab onto my foot or tackle me by surprise, leaving me as a sitting duck to the police currently outdoors. I would look stupid as they laugh and cuff me while applauding the individual who saved the day.

"Everybody in here!" I yell. I point over at the wall furthest away from me, "I want all of you to move to that side of the building."

With the group on that side, nobody could cause me any trouble if one sparked an inclination to do so as I attempt an escape.

Everyone slowly pulls their heads up to see where I am directing them to move. Each person gingerly gets up to obey and makes their way to the side wall where they will huddle together. They all move quietly, and some attempt to soften their cries for fear that I might individually call them out for it.

The more time being wasted outside in conversation, the greater the chance that more police will come to hamper my escape efforts. The two officers talking to Rick are intentionally stalling for time. I must intervene to expedite their decision-making and prevent them from wasting any more of this precious time.

I move with my captive to the right side of the front door, opposite the side I ordered the civilians to relocate. I slide along the wall toward the glass door so that the police outside cannot get a clear shot at me. I pull the hostage in front of me as a human shield, putting him between me and the door.

Before leading my hostage out the transparent front doors, I take one last glance over at the people lined up along the side wall. Almost everyone is indirectly looking at me, trying their best not to establish any eye contact that could start any trouble. They are all genuinely scared, and rightfully should be. Each one cannot wait to get home. They all want to see their wives, husbands, and children on this holiday that was interrupted by violence and fear. They all nervously wait for my departure, a departure that will bring peace back into their lives again. They will go home and be thankful while hugging, kissing, and crying tears of joy over their loved ones. They will escape from here and have a fine holiday with their family members. Well, almost all of them. Everyone except the young girl who lies behind the counter, whose blood still stains my mask and face. What a miserable and depressing time it will be for all those who care about her.

Even though my words will mean nothing to those along the wall, I decide that something needs to be said. I feel the need to lessen the pain I have caused, anything to ease their souls.

"This will be the last time I see all of you. Don't fear me anymore. I cannot hurt you. Once I pass through these doors, I will either escape or be killed. Do not follow me because this bank will now be your sanctuary. Whatever happens outside in the next few moments does not need to involve you. The end is closer than it may seem."

I grip the hostage tightly as I push him out the front door to confront the three policemen outside.

The Bad Guy

CHAPTER 6

"What're you doin'?!" screams one of the policemen behind the cop car.

"You are all wasting my time, so I decided to escape on my own accord," I reply.

"Wait!" cries the same individual. "We can work this out!"

"Humph," I retort. "I know all your sly tactics. You waste time and wait for more backup to come so that you can develop a more effective way to break my chances of escape. Don't play me for stupid! I am getting out of here now."

I sidestep left with the hostage into the slushy lawn out front, using his body to cover me from the three policemen gathered around the second police car.

"What do you want us to do?" an unsure Rick asks me.

"Nothing now," I respond. "I just want all three of you to stand there."

I keep edging my way through the mud, moving in an arc-like path to continue facing the police. As we approach the front police vehicle, I glance over at the back seat. I was correct. The person sitting there is Teddy. His eyes begin darting back and forth between the hostage and me and the police beyond us. He must be wondering what could unravel as the police attempt to deter my escape efforts, or how I might try something to

45

heighten the tension. Teddy knows me well. He knows that I am willing to throw curveballs into a plan to better our outcome.

Luckily, this police car points directly out into the main road without any obstruction. I am going to steal it and make my getaway.

"Give me your car key," I whisper into the captive's ear as we stop next to the driver's door.

I watch his arm quiver as he briskly begins rummaging through his pocket to find what I asked. The speed of this action actually surprises me considering the trance he seemed to be in earlier. I watch his hand. I doubt he will try anything, but I keep a close watch just to make sure.

I hear the sound of jingling as his fingers frisk the inside of his pocket. He pulls out a set of four keys attached to a chain. He flips through each key within his right hand before lifting one of them between his thumb and index finger.

"This one is it," he assures me.

I let go of his uniform for just a moment with my left hand and cross it over my weapon hand to clutch the key from his grasp. I return my hand to grip the same spot on his collar while still holding the key. I give him a small push forward and take a step with him just past the crease of the driver's side door.

I drop my left hand from his collar again and slide the key into the vehicle lock to turn, pull it out, and swing the door open behind us. I grab him one last time and peer over at the three cops pointing their weapons at me, each one studying me intently and awaiting my next move. There is nothing I need to say to them. My actions will tell it all.

I raise my pistol in their direction and wield two shots into the windshield of the police vehicle they surround. At this motion, all three drop down next to the car to avoid my gunfire.

I lower my firearm to my hostage's thigh and fire a single shot through it. *BANG!*

He screams out in agony as I shove him forward to the ground. Directly following the quick shove, I dash into the vehicle and slam the car door shut behind me.

"Keep your head down!" I yell to Teddy in the back seat.

I duck my head and thrust the key into the ignition. Bullets begin raining into our vehicle, smashing through the glass and pelting through metal, thudding with a sound like hail. I thrust the key forward, slam the car into drive, and pound the pedal straight to the floor without picking my head up to look. I am going to drive blind out of this parking lot.

The car lunges forward as we accelerate. I give a short tug on the right side of the wheel to keep our vehicle from getting too close to the building or bank sidewalk. I attempt to visualize the parking lot and the location of the main road. If I keep the car straight, we should be able to dart right through the rest of the lot, out the entrance, and onto the main street.

The car's path is smooth. Our vehicle advances without hitting anything. Are we on the main road yet?

BA-BOOM!!!

The left side of the vehicle hurls into the air before collapsing back down onto its suspension not built for a load like this. Part of the car scrapes the ground on impact with a disturbing sound like that of nails scratching a chalkboard. I take my foot off the gas for an instant to think about what we hit and evaluate our position.

At that high speed, our car probably caught a good piece of the curb next to the entrance. If I am correct, we just entered the main road. I whip the wheel all the way to the left with the assumption that we are on that road.

The rain of gunfire on the vehicle ceases at this point. Whether it is because of empty clips or the astonishment at the sight of my wild driving, it does not matter. It must be safe to sit up for a few seconds, so I pop my head just over the steering wheel to view our car's position relative to the road.

Perfect! Well, not perfect, but good enough. Our car rests in the middle of the road at a slight angle with the head of the car a little to the right. I press on the gas again, hoping that the hard fall did not affect any motor functions of the vehicle. My wish comes true. The car begins to proceed along the road. Keeping my head just low enough to get a glimpse of the street, I grasp the wheel to fine-tune my direction. We need to get out of here fast.

I keep increasing the speed. When I get into the mid-70 mph range, I begin to feel uncomfortable about keeping my head so low while moving. I estimate that the bank is at least a hundred yards behind us. A vital shot killing me now is highly unlikely. Hell, if they put a bullet straight through the back of my head at this distance, I deserve to die. I slide up the seat and settle into a comfortable position to continue the getaway.

I peer into the side-view mirror once my body is adjusted. The second police car behind us at the bank has not come out of the lot to follow us.

"Why'd you shoot that guy?"

I almost forgot that Teddy is back there.

"What?" I reply, not ready for the question.

"The policeman," he says. "I mean, we still could have escaped without the bullet you put through his leg."

"Oh, I see what you're asking. Take a look behind us," I instruct him. "There is nobody there. Right now, the two policemen that would have been chasing us are tending to the other one's wound. He'll be fine and heal. We could've still made it out had I not done that. It just probably would have been harder, especially if they tailed us outta there. You understand?"

"Okay, I see," he responds. "I must've still been kinda out of it and confused a little bit because of what happened back at the bank."

That statement brings up my next question to him. "How did you end up arrested in the back seat of this car?"

I take my gaze off the road ahead and switch it into the rear-view mirror to look at Teddy. He looks exhausted. I have never seen him this burned-out before. Usually, we would all look and feel fatigued after a job, but this is the worst I have ever seen him. I do understand how he must be feeling about this now, though. He was arrested and thrown into the back of a cop car. The police and security cameras have seen his face. He does not have the same luxury of anonymity as I do with the damp mask I still sport. The police now recognize what he looks like and will relentlessly be looking for him if we escape this.

"I dunno," he explains after taking some time to think. "I was in the vault with Sergio when all of a sudden, I lost consciousness. We were finishing up putting the money in the pack when everything went black. Sergio didn't do that to me, did he?"

"Yeah, he fuckin' did!" I quickly interject. "Both he and Marco were in on it! Sergio knocked my ass out too! It's a lot more lucrative to split the loot two ways between brothers than dividing it between the four of us. They left us there to get picked up by the cops!"

"There's no way they'd do that!" Teddy says. "We've known them our whole lives. They wouldn't, no, couldn't do anything like that to us. Never! You're wrong. There has to be a reason why things turned out the way they did."

"I don't think so, Teddy," I say. "I cannot think of any other circumstance where they would knock both of us out, take all of the money, and leave us behind to be captured by the police. I know that we have been friends with them for a long time but think about it, Teddy. What a perfect time to sever a relationship. Right when they can take everything from us and have no repercussions. That is what they were thinking. Well, those repercussions will be coming."

"I cannot believe this!" Teddy exclaims. "I just don't understand it!"

"You've got to be careful with who you trust, man," I lecture him. "Even those that you think are closest to you can be the reason for your demise."

I stop looking back at Teddy and pay attention to the road.

"Well, we can't worry about them now," I tell him. "We aren't safe enough to be discussing things right now."

How appropriate. As I utter those words, a police vehicle on the opposite side of the road appears ahead of us with its lights flashing. I fly right by it and take a look in the mirror as it promptly turns around and accelerates to tail us. Even though we gained a significant amount of ground as it turned, we are still in the proximity of its sights. As long as our car is in view, we are in trouble. The officer will keep track of our location until more and more police join in to help. It will not matter how good of a driver I am. At some point, this will turn out the same way as all the other car chases do on television shows like *COPS*. Trust me, police chases tend not to end well for those being pursued.

I think about the rest of the getaway. The transition spot I planned before the robbery is just about six miles from the bank. It is a mile and a half beyond the gas station that we just flew by.

We need to keep our tail as far back as possible to give us enough time to jump out of the vehicle at the pre-determined spot. This mile and a half will be one hell of a speed race. Our cop car will test its manufactured limits. I press into the pedal and move my body forward into racing position to better focus on the road.

I am pushing about 100 mph already but keep accelerating. Fortunately, the two-lane road does not have too many cars on it given the holiday. We chose a good bank to hit due to the light traffic flow. The speed kicks up to 120 mph. The car will not go too much faster than this. Hell, I do not want it to. The wind is beating so loud against the front windshield that I am starting to get uncomfortable. I skirt around a seemingly motionless car in my lane. I would not be able to maneuver at this speed if the road were not this straight.

After scrambling past a few more vehicles, I see our spot up ahead. I start to tap the brake but then slam my foot down when I determine the speed is safe enough to do so. The car slides and pulls off the side of the road before it finally comes to a complete stop.

Not a split-second passes before I yank the key out of the ignition and launch out the door. I sprint over to Teddy's door to quickly get him out from the back.

Hurry! Hurry! Hurry! I tell myself while not looking up to see how far the police are behind us.

"Let's go!" I yell at him. "Don't worry about the cuffs. We can get those off later."

We dart toward the woods. The stolen ATV sits next to the tree, right where I left it for my escape. Escaping on the ATV was my individual getaway plan, but it will not be a problem having Teddy with me.

"Get on behind me!" I shout to Teddy. "Get your arms over my head and around my waist so you don't fall off!"

He promptly follows the orders as he flings both arms over and around me. I flip the starter switch upward, press the ignition button, and take off down the wooded trail. The police are left in the dirt and snow that shoot up behind us as we disappear into the forest.

CHAPTER 7

We pull into the moderately full parking lot and find a spot that is not in the direct vicinity of our room. If this second vehicle is linked to us, it would not be particularly smart to park directly in front of it. It is highly unlikely that they will follow us back here, but just in case, we must remain careful. Nothing is certain. Just look at how the events of the day have played out thus far.

Teddy and I get out of the car. It is essential that we do not speak to each other until we get to the motel room. I glance around the lot and note that there is only one person at the far end of it. There is no threat in anybody recognizing Teddy's face right now.

This motel is in a remote area, quite a distance away from where the craziness with the bank robbery occurred. It is far from high-end, but much nicer than what one would imagine when thinking of a motel. It is clean, quiet, and even has a small fridge and microwave in the room. This is a great place to lay low for a while.

We make our way along the outside of the building until we find room number 108. I swipe the card and hear the door click as the tiny green light above the handle starts blinking. I swing the door open and make my way across the room to the bed at the far end. I immediately plop down on the end of it. Teddy tails me inside but makes his way over to the mirror on the front wall to observe his face and hair.

"I have some clippers in my bag," I direct, pointing my finger at one of the bags that I brought here yesterday. "You might want to trim up a bit. They are going to catch you quicker if you look like that."

It was unfortunate that Teddy got the mask taken off his face. We purposely grow out the hair on our heads and faces before pulling off any jobs, for fear that one day this might happen. The police will undoubtedly find out who Teddy is, but the drastic change in appearance will make others less likely to recognize him, especially in the next few days. It is always important to give yourself time, even if it is not much. Time is especially important now to sort out the events and intricacies of what happened today.

Teddy makes his way over to the table to grab the shaver out of my bag. He still looks rough. The bags under his eyes are very evident with deep dark circles around them. The earlier frenzy has profoundly affected him. He does not say a word but just finds the clippers and makes his way over to the bathroom.

Before closing the door, I yell over at him. "Hey man, are you alright? You are not looking too well."

"Naww!" he speaks back, "I'm exhausted and not feeling great. I am going to clean myself up, take a shower, and then sleep. I need a little bit of rest before I can think clearly."

"Go right ahead then, Teddy," I say. "It has been one hell of a day. Get yourself cleaned up."

I did not expect to have Teddy staying in the same motel with me. In the original plan, we were all supposed to stay at different places at scattered locations, so if one person was nabbed, the rest would be in good shape. None of us told each other about our own hideout location. That way, nobody could rat out the rest should he get caught. We did not think that any of us would do such a thing to each other but figured it was better to be safe than sorry. That is why it will be difficult, if not impossible, to locate the Celetta brothers now. Looking back, had we decided to tell each other's post-job locations, Marco and Sergio would not have considered knocking Teddy and me out. I guess they could have lied about that too, though.

Yesterday I packed more than enough clothes and food in the room for one person. The reason for my over-packing was due to the uncertain amount of time that I would need to lay low. I tend to overdo or over-anticipate things. I am the kind of person who takes way too much luggage on vacation for fear that I might be short a pair of clothes. In this case, my over-preparedness worked out well for Teddy.

I lie down on the bed and rub the bump that is protruding from my forehead. Even the slightest touch prompts a stabbing pain. What the hell happened today?

Before retracing the situation both Teddy and I find ourselves in because of Sergio and Marco, I plan to review the most recent events to make sure we are in no immediate danger of being caught. I do not want any of the tough decisions and risks that were taken during our spur-of-the-moment getaway to backfire and abruptly end our freedom. I do not want to miss even the smallest detail that could get us caught.

After hopping onto the ATV, we rode through the woods along a trail that was pre-arranged to be my personal getaway route. The stolen car I drove to the bank was supposed to be my ride to the ATV. Due to the unexpected changes in the execution of the bank robbery, taking the cop car on the spot seemed the most viable form of transportation to get me to the trail. In addition to using the police vehicle to escape, I was also able to rescue Teddy.

The brief ATV ride through the woods brought us to a large commuter parking lot where another stolen vehicle sat waiting for our escape. The black SUV was parked in the row closest to the woods so I would not have to worry about someone seeing my sketchy black figure running out from the trees with a mask and not think something of it. That location also offered a quick departure that might have been necessary had someone successfully tailed us through the woods.

Teddy and I had no trouble once we reached the lot. When we got to the edge of the woods, we swiftly hopped off the ATV and made our way into the SUV. The commuter lot had plenty of parked cars but appeared to be void of life when we arrived. I started the car and figured it would be okay to take off my mask, so I ripped it off my face and tossed it into the seat behind us. I had fortunately brought two sets of clothes in the car. I would allow Teddy, still in cuffs, to get dressed in one of these sets that I packed. Wearing different clothing would raise a lot less suspicion from those looking for us in our black robbery gear.

"Throw those on!" I directed Teddy. "Also, check that little leather pack underneath the seat. I might have an extra handcuff key in there."

I was correct. The little pack I stowed under the seat had some useful items I put together a couple of years before. Some of the things included in this pack were a first aid kit, a compass, and a map. Though that pack was too small to contain much, it did have a handcuff key. Again, my overly careful planning was not such a waste after all.

There was no need to hurry after leaving the lot. Breaking the speed limit or drawing any needless attention would have been the only things that could have gotten us caught at that point. I drove the SUV north for approximately 15 miles, taking back roads to avoid the chaotic holiday highway traffic. After a short time, we finally made our way to the next stolen vehicle. That old fifth-generation Honda Civic sat off the road near Carmine's Auto Parts. I chose that location the night before, seeing that other cars were left unattended around that spot. Most of the cars left there were pieces of junk that had "For Sale" signs in the windows. The owners hoped that they could salvage any money from them and not deal with any of their transmission problems or upkeep costs anymore.

We pulled off the road and took our time before we transferred ourselves from the SUV to the Civic. There was a slim chance that someone could catch us at that point, so we were not in a hurry. Teddy, recently handcuff-free, finished getting dressed into the clothes that I told him to put on. I, too, began stripping off my bloodied black robbery uniform and threw on the green sweatshirt and jeans that Teddy handed me. As much as I wanted to keep them on, the last thing I took off were my black gloves. It was better to leave fingerprints around at that point than bring the DNA-stained gloves along with us.

After putting on my new outfit, I scrunched up the crime-stricken attire into a ball. It was still damp with the gore from earlier. I could not get that image out of my head. How far had my crimes gone to have the blood of innocent people on my clothes? Things used to be much simpler when we first decided to embark upon a life of crime. It had not hit me until then just how deep we were in this. I murder innocent people. This is not just a game or a way of living. This is real.

That woman looked right into my eyes as I pulled the trigger. She did not see my face but was able to see me through my eyes. She saw evil, an evil I never quite associated with myself.

I turned the rear-view mirror and stared into my own eyes. What I saw were the eyes of wickedness, the unfathomable fact I never quite grasped. My gaze dropped down the mirror to the rest of my face. My face told a different story. There was a distinct sadness in my reflection. Underneath that mask I was a person, just like that girl.

"Alright, Kevin! Are you all set to go?" Teddy said, breaking my concentration.

"Yeah, let's get going," I answered, pushing open the door. "Don't forget to snag that little leather pack. We might need it again."

Teddy nodded as I headed out and closed the door.

Outside was still rough, even for it being three-something in the afternoon. The sun was not going to come out today as the clouds hung high in the sky to cover it up. I bundled myself up in the sweatshirt as the weather quickly hit my body. I did not remember it being that cold when we took off along the trail on the ATV. I probably did not feel it due to the amount of adrenaline that was prevalent in that frenzied getaway.

"Teddy, before you close the door, give me those clothes," I gestured for the attire that he just took off. "Don't forget the mask I threw back there too."

He handed them over to me, and I bunched them together into the damp ball of my clothes I still held.

"Go to the car and wait while I get rid of these," I said.

He nodded, not saying anything, and lightly jogged toward our next vehicle. I could tell he was cold and did not waste any time after listening to my instructions.

I headed for the line of trees about 50 yards from the vehicles. I looked around the dead wooded area for a soft patch of dirt. The wet snow loosened some of the ground, as I could feel my shoes squish and give a little. I found a sunken area between three trees where their roots did not affect the depth I could dig.

I dropped to my knees and started digging the muddy earth with my hands. The frozen, wet dirt hurt my fingers until they went numb. I stopped when I dug a depth of about a foot and a half. It was deep enough that no animal would dig it up.

I pushed the ball of clothes into the hole and began piling dirt on top of them to hide my sins. The physical evidence may now be gone, but the pain and hurt will live on. There is no way to bury that.

I pressed my shoes on top to flatten the piled dirt and rubbed my hands together in an attempt to get some circulation back. I walked out of the woods to meet Teddy in the Civic.

I sat down on the chilled seat of the car, and my body shivered. We pulled onto the road after hearing the "swish" sound made by the tires as they rolled through the wet snow. We made our way west for about 50 miles until we came to the pre-arranged motel where we currently reside.

So that brings us to now. I continue lying on the bed, not using the slightest amount of energy to pull myself up. It is incredibly relaxing not to exert any physical strain given the fatigue and stress put on my body. I do not want to move or plan on moving anytime soon. I just want to meld into the bed and become a part of it forever.

The subtle roaring of the shower from the bathroom continues as Teddy cleans himself up. I, too, need to take a shower due to the blood and sweat my body accumulated throughout the day. I must be really disgusting right now. It is not my top priority at the moment, as all I want to do is relax.

I outstretch my arms along the bed. Before I can get completely comfortable, the thought of two names distracts me from doing so: Sergio and Marco.

How could they do this to us? Not only did they greedily take the money for themselves, but they also hung us out to dry for the cops. Teddy and I barely got out of there, and we have nothing to show for our efforts. That is right, nothing at all. We put our lives on the line so that they could reap the benefits. Why would they stab us in the back?

I cannot figure it out. For as careful as I am, how could I have let this happen? It completely blindsided me. Sergio knocked Teddy and me out and took off with our money. Those greedy little bastards. They did not care about how long we were friends together. They just turned on us just like that.

It was a ballsy move to leave us for the police, knowing we would spew as much intel as we could on them. They must have known we would not hold back after the very apparent betrayal. There was no way this was spur-of-the-moment. They had to have planned this for some time and figured out a way, in the long-term, not to get caught.

The sound of the shower immediately halts. The fresh-shaven Teddy walks into the room with a towel around his waist. "What clothes should I throw on?"

I thrust my body to sit up at the edge of the bed. "You can wear any of those in the dresser," I point. "It really doesn't matter to me."

"Thanks," he says as he makes his way over and begins to dress.

I have not seen Teddy without facial hair or with short hair for quite some time. He looks young but very different than I remember. The complete transformation made by the haircutting was a good choice, as it will be very difficult for anyone to identify him at a glance. He still looks exceptionally weathered, though, and definitely needs some rest.

"Teddy, whenever you start feeling hungry, you can grab something out of that little fridge. I packed up some different kinds of lunchmeat and those little mini-dinner things in the boxes. Feel free to eat as much as you need. I packed a shit ton."

"Thanks, dude," he says. "I am really not too hungry right now, though. I'm just gonna lay down for a bit and maybe eat something when I wake up."

"That's cool," I respond. "Just to let you know, I may not be here when you wake up."

"What?!" he questions. "There is no way you can go out right now! You know that! What're you gonna do?"

"I'm going to the self-storage to see if Sergio and Marco show up. It may be the only chance we have of finding them," I answer.

"You know that they probably aren't gonna show, right?" Teddy asks.

"I know that! It is worth a shot, though," I say. "They might not have adjusted their plans, thinking we are in jail and not going to show. That might still be the only opportunity for them to meet, assuming they didn't hide out together after the job."

"Alright," he says in an unsure tone. "What're you going to do if you find them there? Are you going to kill them?"

Teddy gazes at me, waiting for the answer. I can tell that he really does not want to know the answer. He would be hurt if I gave the reply I most want to give.

"I don't know," I tell him. "I really do not know. If I need to, I will. We just cannot lose any possible opportunity to find them. This could be our only shot. I don't want to be running around my entire life without this closure. We have to find them."

"I understand," he simply says, not revealing any of his thoughts. "Be careful and don't do something that you will regret."

"Don't worry," I assure. "I'll let you know what's up when I get back. Now get yourself some sleep."

With that settled, Teddy climbs into his bed and bundles himself into a comfortable position. He will be completely passed out in the next couple of minutes.

I work my way into the small bathroom to take a shower and rid myself of all the gore and sweat. Even with the change of clothes that I threw on earlier in our getaway, I still feel extremely disgusting. At least that change of clothes kept the grossness off the end of the bed I laid on.

The bathroom is very humid due to Teddy's shower a short time earlier. The moisture still hangs heavy as the condensation on the big mirror proves. I strip down under the dim light before starting the hot water and stepping in the shower to clean and relax.

The storage facility I am going to is an old one on the edge of a small town. It will take some time to drive there from this motel. When all four of us were planning for this bank job, we collectively decided to meet up at that facility. It is a pretty barren location for the most part and will definitely be so at midnight tonight. We were all supposed to meet there to tie up any loose ends, split up the money, and determine when and if we could show our faces in public again.

As Teddy hinted, I still believe it is a useless endeavor, but I would never forgive myself if I were to let this slip by me.

I pick up the mini shampoo bottle off the shelf and squeeze it until enough of the runny liquid comes out to cleanse my hair.

I then think about what Teddy asked me. Am I going to kill Sergio and Marco? What am I going to do? Am I really willing to murder two of my former best friends? With all the rage filling within me, the idea of murder as punishment bothers me. I want to know why they did this to me, why they would do such a thing. What will I do if they are to show up? I cannot just walk straight over to them and ask them because they might be afraid and put a bullet between my eyes. They stabbed me in the back once already, so what is to prevent them from finishing me off for good? Neither of them has killed before, but I do not know if they are willing to do it now. I do not understand them or their thinking at all. I thought I knew everything about Sergio and Marco and could trust them, but their actions today completely threw me off. I cannot trust those closest to me now.

They did me wrong, and they need to pay. I need to be the one in control of the situation if I am to see them tonight. If killing is the best way to set things right, then I should be content to use it as a means. I am not the one who stabbed someone in the back. I did not leave them on the bank floor to be caught and greedily take all the money for myself. If they are to die, they did it to themselves.

A mixture of anger and excitement begins to flood over me. They deserve to die, and I am the only one who can make that happen. How appropriate would it be to take them out in vengeance after being left for dead? Things like this do not happen in real life. This situation seems like it could be a plotline in a movie. I have a chance to be that person, that someone who prevails with all odds against him. Teddy and I will get our pride and money back. What a perfect ending that will be. Who cares if they were once our friends? They made it quite clear that they did not cherish our friendship enough.

I twist the water nozzle off and grab one of the small white towels to dry. I am fresh and clean now. After drying off, I head into the room to get some warm clothes from the dresser. Through the blinds, I can already tell that it is pitch-black outside. Teddy is fast asleep with the covers pulled up to his neck and his mouth wide open to breathe. Because of his fresh new haircut, his smooth forehead glistens in the reflection of the motel light. I throw on what I think are some warm clothes and make sure to put on a thick jacket and hat. It is going to be brutally cold this Christmas Eve night.

I head over to the tiny fridge and take out a few slices of lunchmeat to munch on as a snack before taking off. I decide on sliced ham, which I roll into a stick and take some bites. I am not really that hungry. I will eat something more filling when I get back. My thoughts of the day continued to stay with me, preventing me from having an appetite. I am surprised considering how hungry I was this morning.

I head over to the door and take one more good look at Teddy, who is motionless and tranquil in peace.

"Goodnight," I whisper to him before turning around to leave into the arctic night.

CHAPTER 8

The snow begins to fall again, drifting softly to the already white surface. It does not fall hard or dance wildly as it does sometimes but just floats vertically to the ground with each speck moving at an equally slow velocity. Upon hitting the ground, the fresh flakes create a new thin layer of powder over the hardened ice from the snow that partially melted earlier in the week.

My eyes enjoy the sight of such a beautiful and calm wintry night. An eerie silence swept over the surrounding setting when I arrived, aiding me so I could hear my thoughts clearly and feel a part of the environment around me. I am probably the only living thing within miles of this spot, not seeing any squirrel or vehicle pass since I got here.

I chose a spot on the darker side of one of the storage units, shielding me from view if Sergio or Marco were to come. The only gleam of light comes from the moon above, reflecting upon the resting white snow. Flakes begin forming a pile around my legs, but I just let them bury me as I lean my back against the cold metal unit. The night is a frigid one, one that makes people chill to their core. Initially, I was in pain, shivering from such a harsh temperature. It does not bother me anymore, though. At a certain point, the cold numbed away all the feeling in my body, leaving behind a comfortable sensation of frozen relief. I sit here, sleepily fading away into my surroundings.

I am as alone as alone can be. People are already snuggled up tight in their beds with feelings of joy and happiness. They are full from their home-cooked meals and tired from an enjoyable time sitting by the fire. I am the only person out here in this wintry wonderland. I am the only person who cannot let the hardships of the day pass and live blissfully happy while waiting for the Lord's coming.

Teddy is now my only form of family. He, too, is fast asleep at the motel, putting away the unfortunate events of the day. I hope his dreams bring him comfort. He should have had better. Teddy was always such a good kid who seemed to be pulled into the group's wrongdoings. He should be at home with a family that loves him, where he can wake up without a sad imitation of a Christmas dinner or hide away from something that was not really his fault. Sergio and I are responsible for getting him into this situation in the first place.

Sergio and Marco. I again remind myself of the current situation. This is the first time I can actually think clearly and contemplate the events of today. Has greed seriously brought them to where they are as people right now? I always knew Sergio and Marco would stand firm for things in which they believed, but I would never have guessed that they would be blatant backstabbers. Has this lifestyle of criminal activity melded them into different people?

I immediately freeze this train of thought. Has this lifestyle changed me too? Again, the eyes of the frightened girl flash through my mind. The tender radiant human life was dropped by *my* hand. I have gone too far. Years ago, I would not have even considered such an act. How did this happen to me? Why has life recently become valueless in my conscious mindset? I have accepted this path of criminal activity fairly effortlessly without remorse but find myself murderous without a clear intention to be so. Does a life of crime inherently lead to violent behavior? Could this "slippery slope" also be the reason why Sergio and Marco became so greedy as to backstab Teddy and me? Perhaps the ramifications of living this criminal life have gradually turned us all into monsters.

Maybe we have pushed this too far. We would never have imagined an outcome like this in the beginning. I cannot believe we just knocked over a federal bank with a disastrous ending that cost a woman her life and caused the distress of other innocent people who will never forget what happened. I am done with this. I have had enough of this "entertaining and pulse-pounding" kind of life. Living in the moment and having a chance at a slight monetary advancement all ends in misery anyway.

This behavior needs to stop before my personality contorts into an even worse state (if that is possible at this point). My lack of regard or recognition of this way of life will end tonight. I hate who I am. Nothing about this is enjoyable.

I look up at the barren road from which the Celettas will probably not appear. I do not have a plan if they are to show. Am I really going to kill them? Would that be a fair solution? I do not know. What am I to do? I only want to get the money back for Teddy and me. That seems to be the only suitable solution. How am I to get it back without this threat of violence, though? I do not know the answer to that question.

My weapon lies in my hand. I pull it into my lap and inspect its cold metal body that has flakes swiftly covering it. I never took the time to think about this simple, interesting instrument before. The science surrounding this small device is fascinating. Unlike several other innovations that are made for the betterment of human life, this is one of the few with the sole purpose of destroying it. This truly is a mechanism of death.

This little piece of dark hardware does not seem too menacing, though. At first sight, its sleek body and simple parts do not elicit any murderous inclinations. This hunk of metal is merely an item. The real sources of death are those that hold such a weapon and make those decisions. The gun itself just obeys whoever is operating it. I view the hand attached to the weapon. It is mine. I was the one who murdered those people. It was not the piece of metal forcing me to do so. In the end, there are no excuses. Those decisions were entirely mine.

I tuck the gun away. My body is completely covered up to my torso in snow as I sit leaning back against the wall. It does not matter that Sergio and Marco are not coming. I am neither in the mood to move nor in a hurry to get out of here. This soft, lonely, wintry wonderland creates a strange, yet refreshing, feeling of complacency.

So much has happened today. It was entirely too long, and physically and mentally intensive. My body is already at ease in this arctic tundra. Perhaps it is time for my mind to be at ease too. There is no need to worry about Sergio and Marco. They are not going to show tonight. We have no understanding as to where they might be anyway. Because Teddy and I were not involved in their post-bank job locations, we have probably seen the Celetta brothers for the last time.

I was infuriated before I left the motel to come out here tonight. The atmosphere has calmed me down quite a bit since then. We probably will not see the brothers or the money again, but it does not matter. Both Teddy and I got away with our lives. Though our goal was entirely different, things could have turned out significantly worse. I am on this earth another day to fight on and figure this whole "life" thing out. I sure hope that Teddy's and my situation will square away here soon enough. Things are a mess now, especially with the need to hide from the public eye as a result of Teddy being seen. It will take work to correct, but staying calm and playing it smart will undoubtedly keep us in a good position. That is way more important to us now than the Celetta brothers dilemma.

I brush the snow off of my watch. Due to the darkness surrounding me, I have to study it closely to view the time. Both hands are pointing up. *Merry Christmas*, I internally say sarcastically before releasing a slight chuckle. Not too many people would find themselves here on this particular night. Everyone is tucked away with their pleasant dreams. Here I sit, slowly being buried in a frozen grave in the middle of nowhere on an almost empty stomach. This is what I chose. This is the price I have to pay given this lifestyle. I cannot reverse it or turn back time. Never again will I share in the excitement of the holiday, surrounded by family and content with how things are. That is pure happiness and joy. Not the short-lived thrill induced by the crap I do.

I need to get out of here. I will freeze in my self-reflection if I stay. I stand up and brush the settled snow off of me. I look to the dead road as I brush. They are not coming. They are too smart for that. I head to my vehicle with the only sound coming from the crunching snow under my feet. I have to get back and invest in some much-needed sleep.

The Bad Guy

CHAPTER 9

I kept running toward Teddy's house through the intense heat on that blazing summer day. My anger for the Celetta brothers faded significantly with the increased fatigue and perspiration that my body endured. Much of my shirt was drenched in sweat. Though I was not too far from his house when I started running, the temperature made my half of a mile seem like twenty times that amount.

When the house came into view, I crossed the street after checking to see if any cars were coming. Like the lack of people outside, no one seemed to be out driving either. It was almost spooky the way that no life was going on around the neighborhood. I would have called it a ghost town had the neighborhood depicted the other traits I always pictured in one. I imagined a ghost town to be lifeless but also envisioned it to have dark, frightening houses situated beneath gloomy clouds. That is why my definition of ghost town would not work for those nice suburban houses on that notably radiant day.

When I got to Teddy's house, I stopped for a moment to catch my breath. I placed my hands on my knees as I sucked in the toasty air. My insides were recovering from the exercise I forced upon them.

Why had I run so hard? There was no need to push myself through the pain and stifling weather. If I had not run, the ice cream I had eaten earlier would have been sufficient enough to keep myself cool. I ran to avoid conflict. I lost the will for confrontation created by the heated debate with Sergio and Marco and the scuffle with Crevan before that. I was still angry at that point, but I did not want to fight anymore. Running was the only way to dissipate the built-up fury within.

I composed myself after I felt the energy to do so and began walking up Teddy's driveway. When I got to the concrete path leading to the porch, an immediate sensation of refreshing coolness passed over my body. As the sun passed behind the house, I stepped into the shade. The fresh shade, along with the rest from the workout, put me into an instant state of relaxation. This refreshment gave me a newfound perception of contentment as I stepped onto the porch and knocked on the front door.

It took a couple of seconds before someone inside recognized my presence. I heard a clattering of footsteps across the wooden floor to reach the front door. The door flung open and Teddy's mother was there to greet me.

"Hi there, Kevin!" she smiled. "How have you been?"

Teddy's mom, a short, pleasant woman, always greeted me kindly when I came over. She loved guests and found me quite a suitable friend and mentor for her son.

"I'm doing pretty good," I lied but said respectfully. "How have you been?"

"Oh, you know," she answered, "I'm doin' just fine. I've been taking care of all those chores needed done around the house."

Before wandering into a more detailed discussion about both of our lives, I cut straight to the reason for being there. "I was wondering if there is any way I could talk to Teddy?"

"Sure!" she said. "He ran in crying and shot straight to his room. I tried to talk to him and see what happened, but he refused to speak to me."

She led me inside. "You are his best friend, Kevin. You go talk to him and make him feel better."

"Don't worry," I assured her. "I'll go up and talk to him. He'll be fine."

"Thank you," she said softly. "You do mean a lot to him, ya know?"

I looked directly into her eyes. "Yes, I know."

I knew this all along. Teddy looked up to me as his big brother. I was the one person in this world that he respected over anyone. Even his mother could not console him the way I knew I could. That is what brought me over there. I needed to be the person to lead him, the one to explain and justify the reasons for why things turned out the way they did earlier that day. I never chose to be this important or influential to him, but since he somehow decided it would be that way, I felt the responsibility to mold him into the best person he could be. I wanted him to be a better person than me, the epitome of the person I ought to be.

I began to climb the stairs before Teddy's mom stopped me, "Hey Kevin, do you want me to put something together for you to eat? I have a lot of salami in the fridge."

"No, I'm fine. But thank you," I responded as I continued to ascend up the steps.

Now my sweat-soaked shirt stuck uncomfortably to my chest inside the air-conditioned house. The sudden extreme drop in temperature gave me a sharp chill. It would be some time before my body adjusted to the dramatic change.

Teddy's door was not far from the top of the staircase. I approached the shut door down the hallway on the right and gave a solid three knocks on it. "Hey Teddy, it's me! Can I come in?"

I patiently waited until he shuffled over, turned the knob, and slowly pushed the door open to let me inside. He did not say a word and only looked down at the carpet as he turned around to sit back down on his dark-blue comforter. I followed behind him, grabbed the wooden chair by his desk, and dragged it around so I could sit and chat with him.

I lowered myself down on the hard chair and was able to see the wetness on his cheeks from the tears that had not yet dried from his face. The light coming through the window shone directly on his somber face. He had been crying but must have abruptly stopped upon my arrival to keep from feeling ashamed. He just sat there, occasionally gasping as a result of excessive sobbing.

"I came over here to check up on you, bud," I said. "Are you feeling alright?"

He nodded unconvincingly, continuing to look down at a spot on the floor.

"Why'd you run away?" I asked.

Teddy did not answer right away but instead clenched his jaw in deep concentration. He did not know what to say and was trying to come up with an honest explanation.

"I was scared," he eventually admitted. "…and I did not know what to do. Marco and Sergio were telling me to fight, and you were telling me not to. I was just so confused and afraid."

"There's no reason to be afraid, man," I added. "You should have just done what you wanted to do. Did you want to fight Crevan?"

"No, I did not want to fight at all," he responded. "But I want all of you guys to like me too. Crevan probably would have kicked my butt. I just couldn't take it."

"Who cares what Sergio thinks?" I told him. "Who cares what Marco thinks? Hell, who actually cares about what I think either? The only thing that matters is what you think is the right thing to do. Sometimes you just have to listen to yourself."

Teddy lifted his eyes from the ground and peered into mine. His brown eyes were glassy from the teardrops still in them.

"Ya see?" I pointed out. "I knew you did not want to fight him. I knew he was going to kick your butt if you guys ended up fighting. I just wanted to look after you. I knew you wanted to get away from there, so that's what I hoped you would do. There was no need to fight with Crevan. You knew that."

"Are Sergio and Marco mad?" he asked.

"Not at you!" I assured. "They are a little angry with me, though. I let them know I wasn't happy with what they were trying to do with you."

"So, you were mad at them?" he asked.

"I was," I confessed. "But it'll be fine. I just got so angry at them and went off on 'em a little bit."

"Everything is still fine, though, right?" he questioned.

Though I was upset earlier and even said I did not want to be their friends, after calming down, I knew that fighting with them was just stupid. The Celettas are not bad, their intentions and actions are just misunderstood. All four of us were going to be okay. Our friendship was not over yet. For Teddy's sake, I would make it all work out.

"Yeah," I replied to him. "We'll be fine. That scuffle between us earlier was nothing. I'll call them up to play football or something tomorrow, and everything will be okay. Don't worry about it!"

I did not want to upset Teddy by going into detail about the altercation between myself and the Celetta brothers, so I quickly changed the subject. "Did you want any more ice cream? I promised you that I would get you some more from my house if you wanted any."

"Oh no!" he shook his head. "I was filled up. I don't think I could've even finished the one I had."

He placed his hand on his stomach to indicate that he had enough.

"That's good!" I said. "It is just a shame that stupid kid had to knock it out of your hand. He got what he deserved, though."

I could tell that Teddy was thinking to himself when I brought up the ice cream incident. His mind was working as his brown eyes squinted and stared out the window.

"It looks like you're thinking about something. What is it?" I asked.

"Umm… not really anything." He looked over at me. "I was just wondering why Crevan would want to bother me. We were just walking back and minding our own business. It isn't fair that our good time together had to be ruined by him."

I paused for a moment before answering. I began to think about it too. How did such an awful day come from something that was almost perfect? I did not know how to respond to Teddy. Why can't life be fair? We did nothing to spark such a conflict. It just seemed to happen to us randomly.

Teddy was staring at me, patiently waiting for the advice he knew he could always count on. Any advice that I would give he would hold onto tightly. For some reason, anything that I said always seemed right to him. I was his wise older friend, like an insightful sage that would not let him down.

"My parents always told me that life isn't fair," I began. "Things seem to happen to people without any real explanation. Sometimes bad people get away with things while good people are hurt and stepped on. The only thing that we can do is take things in stride and keep trying. We have to take everything out of life that we can. Life will push you down again and again if you let it. You just have to find your own thing, something that keeps you alive, something that is justifiable in this unfair world. Sometimes people will let you down, but that's okay. You just have to take something back for yourself. You have to be your own man and live for yourself."

Teddy sat there, staring at me intently while holding onto my every word. He understood what I was telling him. I was a great mentor, the terrific older brother that was not blood-related.

"You'll be fine," I told him as I got off the chair. "You feeling any better?"

"I really am," he said and smiled at me. "I'm actually kinda hungry now, but not for ice cream. Wanna go downstairs and get something to eat?"

"Ahh, not really. I kind of need to get back home to take a shower. I'm not really all that hungry yet, but you go on ahead get some dinner downstairs."

Teddy popped up off of his bed. He was emotionally sound and well over the sadness he had just a short time before.

Teddy followed as I moved the chair that I recently occupied back over to its original position and made my way to the door.

"I wanna play some hockey tomorrow," he stated as we walked down the stairs together. "Do you want to do that too?"

"Yeah, sure," I told him. "We haven't done that in a while. That'd be pretty fun."

I made my way over to open the front door and exit to go home. Teddy's mother overheard us talking on our way down the stairs and made her way into the foyer to see how the discussion was going between us.

"Oh, I appreciate your coming over to talk with him," she said.

"It was no problem," I assured her.

"Hey, Teddy!" I called to him before leaving.

He hurried over in response to the call.

"Take it easy, little dude. I'll see you tomorrow. We'll call Marco and Sergio, and we'll play some games. Now go get something to eat."

I put out my hand for a low five, and he immediately smacked it.

"Alright," he said, smiling before running off into the kitchen. "I'll see you tomorrow!"

"Bye," I said to him and his mother before leaving.

"Oh, bye sweetheart," she answered. "Thanks for coming over and have a safe walk back home."

I shut the front door behind me and jumped off of the porch into the front yard. The sky looked a beautiful orange as the sunlight began to set on that hot day. Though it was still hot, it was not unbearable. Even though the day was not one of my favorites, it ended with a sense of satisfaction. I helped comfort and mentor a good friend and planned to mend the friendship with the Celettas the next day. I helped restore what was almost lost.

CHAPTER 10

I wake up to find my body surrounded by several soft motel pillows. I do not sit up right away or open my eyes. My entire body is sore and still exhausted from the stress of the previous day. The swollen bruise atop my head is tender and slightly heavy from the significant amount of blood within it. I pick up my left arm to explore the wound through touch.

"Ow!" I proclaim after gently prodding the contusion. I really should not be messing around with this injury just yet.

"Merry Christmas," Teddy promptly says, realizing that I am indeed awake following my yelp.

I decide to force myself to sit up and commit to staying awake. "Merry Christmas," I reply to him.

I clear the sleep from my eyes and see a clean and dressed Teddy sitting in a chair across the room from me. He sports a black polo shirt and khaki pants. He is nicely outfitted and must have gotten some much-needed rest. However, he still looks aged with a sullen face and has bags under his eyes. The shaving of his head changed his appearance significantly, but even without hair, he seems different somehow. The lively and youthful enthusiasm that I have always known him to display is nowhere visible today.

"How long have you been up?" I ask him.

"I dunno," he responds. "Probably like an hour or so."

"You okay?" I question.

"Yeah, I'm fine," he assures. "I was just sitting here and thinking about the situation I am in. I mean, the whole police looking for me thing."

"You'll be alright," I say. "We just have to take things slowly and be careful about what we do. That's it. We have roughly discussed what to do in a time like this. You know what I am talking about. The main thing we have to do is be smart. Any minor, but still reckless move can put us in a world of hurt."

"I really do think we'll be alright," he answers. "It just feels kinda weird now. Everything is different. We can't live life like we used to. Also, we lost two longtime friends at the same time. So much has happened in one day. I just feel strange."

I attempt to lift his spirit. "Don't worry, things will only get better. We are probably never going to see Sergio and Marco again. With a little time and a few changes, nobody will recognize you, and you'll be free to walk around safely in public again."

"Eh, okay," Teddy says unenthusiastically, looking down and thinking about something intently.

After a short pause, Teddy looks up at me and starts talking again. "Speaking of Marco and Sergio, I assume you didn't see them at all last night, did you?"

"You're right," I shrug. "It was probably for the better, though. I don't know what I would have done if they had shown. They got away with both the money and stabbing us in the back, but we got away with our lives. It is over, and there is nothing we can do about it now. As I said just a second ago, we probably won't ever see them again. We have no leads or any means of contacting them. We have no idea where they might be. We should not even worry about it anymore."

"Really?" Teddy becomes puzzled. "Yesterday you were infuriated with them. What's the reason for your change of heart?"

"I had time outside in the snow to cool off yesterday and really think things over. My heart was racing, and my emotions were all over the place after the job yesterday, so I wasn't able to think clearly. We have to be realistic with our expectations. Sometimes it is just not worth it."

"So you really aren't angry at all anymore?" he asks.

"I'm still very disappointed with how everything turned out yesterday," I respond, "but I shouldn't let that frustrate me too much. Marco and Sergio mean nothing to us now. What do you think? Are you mad at them?"

"To tell you the truth," Teddy says, "I am furious right now. They took everything from me. Not only was it the money, but my freedom and way of living. Their greed put me into this situation even after all the respect and dedication I have shown them over the years. Our friendship meant nothing to them. I seriously thought we were all good friends. I still believe they made such a horrible decision and they should pay for it."

There is a sharpness in his eyes. He did not stutter but spoke clearly to me.

"I care about you, Teddy," I say. "You will never see me do anything of that nature to you. You know that. I went out of my way to retrieve you from the police. I know that everything with the Celettas didn't work out how we wanted it to, but their friendship never was as good as ours. You know that to be true, don't you?"

"I really do," he agrees. "You have always been good to me, Kev, and I really appreciate that. I know that what we have is much stronger than anything either of us had with Sergio and Marco. That still doesn't deny the fact that what they did makes me so angry."

For being so angry, he did a very good job of not showing it. His casual demeanor and relaxed body showed no signs of immense hate or rage.

I climb out of bed and find some jeans from the dresser drawer and a navy polo to throw on. I probably will not spend much, if any, time outside today, so this choice of attire will suffice in this heated motel room.

"You have anything to eat while I was sleeping?" I change the subject.

"I had two Chewy bars this morning when I first got up, but I am still pretty hungry. I haven't had a real meal for a while now."

"Get something out of the fridge," I say. "We have plenty of food in here to chow down on."

Teddy clenches the right part of his jaw and cocks his head to the side. "Ummm... I know you are probably not going to like this idea, but I have an offer for you today."

I glance over at the uncomfortable Teddy about to pitch his plan.

"It is Christmas and all, and I thought we should do something special like go out and get something to eat for lunch instead of throwing lunchmeats together or eating out of boxes. We will have plenty of time to do that in the upcoming days."

I am shocked. How could Teddy want to do something so dangerous? I just expressed how volatile our situation is and how any potential risk can put us in jeopardy.

"That is a terrible idea, Teddy," I say. "We just talked about taking things slowly for the next couple of days, didn't we? It definitely isn't safe for you to show face now. Stuff is probably all over the news about the robbery yesterday, so people will be on the lookout for anything strange. I don't even know how much information investigators might have on us now. We were as careful as we could've been yesterday, but who knows if the police found anything linking the event to us and around this location?"

"I understand that," Teddy responds, showing that his idea was not due to ignorance. "I mean, what are the chances that going out just once will get us caught? Probably pretty slim."

"Not as slim as staying here would be," I argue.

"I really want to go out though," Teddy continues. "Let's make a deal. We won't go to any sit-down places. We'll just go to a gas station or quick fast food restaurant that is open and get something to go. I don't even have to go inside. I'll wait inside the car while you go pick something out."

I contemplate Teddy's request. It is a stupid idea, but at the same time, it will be kind of depressing sitting inside today. Neither Teddy nor I have ever experienced a lackluster Christmas. We have always been surrounded by family or some sort of excitement. He must want this so that he has something to look forward to today. He wants any semblance to the feeling that he is accustomed to on this holiday. Even though this idea is not a smart choice, I owe him this little bit of satisfaction. He needs something to feel good about after the series of unfortunate events.

"I'm not overly excited about this," I say, "but going out might not be too horrible of an idea."

A little smile appears on Teddy's face. "Thanks man, I know it really isn't much, but it is a big thing for me."

"Yeah, I figured," I said. "But don't get too excited about this. It'll be a quick trip. I am just going to run in, grab some sandwiches, burgers or whatever, and get back here immediately."

"I understand and will be fine with that," he assures.

"Where should we go?" I ask while grabbing two jackets out of the closet near the door.

"I don't really care," Teddy answers. "I recall seeing a few shops on the way here. There was a gas station with a nice-looking convenience store down the road. I remember seeing a Chinese food restaurant and a McDonalds a little further back too."

"No Chinese food," I say. "They take too long, and you know that I'm not really a big fan. I'm not feeling any fast food either. How about trying out the little gas station convenience store? If they don't carry any nice subs or pre-made meals, we'll try elsewhere."

"Sure!" he agrees. "That would be perfect."

I knew that anything we might get at that store would probably be the same type of foods we already have here (chips and lunchmeat, etc.), but Teddy did not argue. I suspect he is only looking forward to going out.

"I assume that you are ready to go right now?" I say.

"Yeah, I am," Teddy says. "I'm getting pretty hungry."

I hand him one of the jackets as I put mine on.

I check the digital clock on the bed stand. It is already 1:20. I slept for a long time last night and starting to get pretty hungry now too. As I continue thinking about it, going out is really not that bad. His idea is beginning to win me over. It will give us something to do instead of being confined to this small room all day.

"Ready to go?" he says while throwing the jacket on.

"Alright! Let's do it then," I say while scanning the room for anything else we might need. "Oh yeah, let me bring this just in case."

I walk over to the dresser and open the top drawer. Inside are some socks and on top of them is my pre-paid cell phone. I grab the phone and shove it into my pocket.

"I don't have any numbers in it, but it won't be bad to have on me I guess," I tell Teddy. "I can give you the number to it in case you need me at any time."

I pull out a sheet of paper to write down the number.

"Haha!" Teddy laughs. "Instead of writing it down, let me just put it into my pre-paid phone."

Teddy pulls out a phone from his pocket.

"You have that on you?" I ask. "I told everyone not to bring a phone with them to the bank. I know it isn't a big deal since we all don't have each other's numbers, but that's one extra thing you had to bring with you."

Earlier, when we planned the bank robbery, I had told everyone to keep their phones at their individual getaway locations.

"I know," Teddy says, "I accidentally forgot to leave it there the previous night so I brought it with me the next morning. Look, though, it is nice that I have it so that we can exchange numbers now. I am lucky that with all the craziness that went down at the bank, the police somehow didn't find it on me and take it when I got arrested."

I am a bit agitated that he had it on him, but I guess there is nothing I can do about that now. At least it did not negatively impact anything. I dictate the number for Teddy to put into his phone and he gives me his number.

"I guess that kind of worked out," I say. "Now we can find each other if we somehow get separated."

"Yeah, that's true," Teddy responds. "Now let's get going. I'm getting pretty hungry and ready to go."

I agree with the antsy Teddy but make sure to collect the room key and grab some money before heading out. As soon as I pass through the room door, I immediately stop and turn back around before it closes.

"I need my gun," I say quietly. "I feel uncomfortable without it and probably shouldn't leave it sitting out in the open."

I walk over to where I left it on the nightstand next to my bed.

"I have another one in the bottom dresser drawer, Teddy," I say to him. "I'll give it to you if you feel like you need it."

Teddy pauses and thinks about it. I am confident that if I offer the weapon to him, he will not take it, but I offer it anyway.

"Sure," he answers. "I'll take it for safety. Thanks!"

His answer surprises me. Teddy does not care much for guns and only brings his with him on jobs because we force him to do so. I suppose he is feeling a bit paranoid about the police having seen his face and wants the gun for security.

I walk over to collect the weapon for Teddy, hand it to him, and then tuck my own gun under my jacket before leaving.

CHAPTER 11

I turn our stolen Honda Civic out from the motel parking lot and onto the main road. I almost stop before we pull onto the street because I begin to regret the decision to go out. It was not even a day ago that we were out and almost got ourselves captured and killed. I have yet to check out any news reports to see what the police are looking for at this time. I consciously disregarded the carefully-planned safety measures. We are just asking to get caught right now. I know how much this means to Teddy, but I decide to express my paranoia openly in hopes of changing his decision.

"I think we should turn around, park, and go back inside," I tell him. "I will be honest with you. I am extremely uncomfortable with this right now."

Teddy turns his head and studies me for a split second.

"You really are worried about this, aren't you?" he says. "You have nothing to fear. Look at me. I feel alright, and the police actually know what I look like. We'll be fine. Hell, if we can escape a situation like yesterday almost unscathed, we can probably get away with just about anything now."

I shift my eyes off the road for a moment to look at him. He appears content right now. I would say that he looks more comfortable now than when I first woke up and saw him. I guess this trip really will make his day. I just hope he does not become too reckless or carefree with this newfound confidence.

The weather outside is not quite beautiful, but it is not as brisk as it has been over the past few days. It has stopped snowing for the moment, and the amount that has already accumulated on the ground is not ready to melt just yet. The sky is full of gray clouds that block out any amount of sunlight. Even without the sun, the blanket of snow creates a faint surreal glow over the landscape. The lack of wind and precipitation gives the scenery an eerie stillness. The gloominess surrounding the stillness seems anticipatory as if it is patiently awaiting something.

"Teddy," I break in again. "You didn't happen to catch any news about the events yesterday, did you? Anything at all?"

"Sorry bud," he replies. "I really haven't followed up on that just yet. I guess we'll have to see what's going on when we get back."

I am always a little nervous until I hear or read the news updates on our robberies. Though the media does not give too much away in the investigation aspect of our crimes, it is somewhat soothing to hear them directly say what types of things they know. It gives me satisfaction to see that they are not hiding anything from the public. The fact that they state what kinds of things people should be looking for lets me know that law enforcement is asking the public for assistance. This makes me think that they do not have any major leads at that particular point in time. It will also let us know what to hide if they are looking for a specific clue.

"We're just going to that gas station we passed along this road yesterday, right?" Teddy asks.

"That's correct," I reply. "That is the closest one I know of. If there isn't a good food selection, we'll find something close by."

Maybe it is not a good idea to go to a gas station near our motel. If this particular vehicle or license plate is currently being looked for and spotted at this station, police will certainly search our motel nearby. Checking any news updates would have been very helpful right now.

These combinations of risks that I normally do not take make me uneasy. I attempt to calm myself down. We are going to be out for a maximum of twenty minutes. If I can just make it through this little interval, everything is going to be okay. I bite onto my lower lip. I need to think about the situation at hand.

The gas station is about three miles down this road and will be on our left. We will be there shortly. I will move swiftly and be conscious of the surroundings while I am in there. I will quickly analyze the people that are around and make sure they are not showing any signs of suspicion. Police are another thing to look out for. Some will likely be dispatched to this area even though the crime took place a considerable distance from here.

I might be hyping myself up way too much for this. Teddy is right. Nothing should happen on this simple trip. Being careful and apprehensive is who I am. I really do overanalyze these situations. I should just let this little event transpire and not worry about all the possible outcomes. I do not need any more stress.

"What kind of food are you looking for me to get?" I move to the next topic on my mind, attempting to dispel my uncertainties.

"I dunno," Teddy responds honestly. "Sometimes places like that have little chicken sandwiches or wings and such. They might not have them today, though, since it is Christmas. It really doesn't matter to me."

I glance over and see him searching out the window. His eyes move with his thought process.

"Don't get me any of those cheap hot dogs, though," he continues. "I'm not really in the mood for any of those. Gas station hot dogs are gross."

"I'll check out what things they have when I get inside," I follow. "Don't worry, I'll try to get us something good."

As I finish my sentence, our vehicle pulls past the last part of the ever-stretching line of trees.

"There it is," I blurt out as we both gaze out the window to our left.

There are six cars at the gas station. Two are filling up at the pump while four others are parked in front of the building. It is not too busy, and best of all, there are no police vehicles around. The station itself is relatively secluded in that there are no other shops or stores around it. All that surrounds the building is the vast wilderness. I regain composure and confidence as I view the non-threatening site before me. This trip will be fine.

"I think I'm going to fill up the tank while we're here," I tell Teddy. "Our car needs to be topped off with gas if something goes wrong. We can't make too many trips while we are out. I say that since we are here, we should just do it now. Hell! Who knows if we are going to get into another car chase at some point? We wouldn't want to be caught due to a lack of fuel."

Teddy nods his head with approval and seems to understand my new sense of calm.

I pull our car up to the second pump from the right.

"I'll be back shortly," I tell Teddy. "Keep a lookout and make sure everything is alright."

"Alright," Teddy says, sitting up in the vehicle and looking at me attentively. His eyes are wide and staring deep into mine now. His expression is one of concern, much different from what it has been the majority of this trip. "Be careful, and I'll see you soon."

I shut the door and make my way around the car to the pump. I glance over at Teddy. Teddy's earlier coolness and relaxed attitude must have left him when I parked the car. He is looking all around, studying the people, and specifically keeps an eye on the back road for any sign of trouble. He now clearly understands that putting ourselves out in the public eye is risky.

As I divert my eyes from him to the pump, I know that there is no way I can use my credit card out here. My name cannot be associated with this location, especially when it connects me to Teddy. I will have to pay cash inside for the gas.

I slowly move to the store as I continue thinking about what I should purchase. It will be faster to get the food and pay for the gas at the same time, so I do not have to face the cashier twice.

I peer into the store to see if I can get an idea of what kind of food items they sell before entering. It is a pretty large store that must have a sandwich station and...

No way.

I freeze in place midway to the building. My train of thought is cut short because of what I see through the glass inside. I see Marco Celetta.

The Bad Guy

CHAPTER 12

How did this happen? Out of all the places he could be, Marco stands not even a hundred feet away from me. I continue to look through the glass. I decide that it is definitely him. He is standing by one of the shelves close to the cashier, rocking back and forth with his arms crossed. He appears to be waiting for someone. His expression shows that of impatience and worry, bouncing around like he wants to get out of there.

Out here in the cold, I begin to walk backward to our vehicle slowly. I do not think he has noticed me yet. I need to get out from the open in case his eyes drift in my direction. I turn around quickly and hastily step to the car door. In one motion, I swing open the door, sit, and close it again.

"What is wrong?" a worried Teddy reacts to my bizarre behavior.

"Marco is inside!" I say, pointing my finger to where my eyes are fixed.

"Are you serious?" He jolts his head to look for himself. "Oh my God!"

"What were the chances of running into him again?" he asks. "You just told me an hour ago that we are probably not ever going to see the Celettas again, and here is Marco, right in front of our eyes."

A moment passes as Teddy and I let this surprise sink in.

"What should we do?" Teddy finally asks the obvious question.

"I don't know," I say. "We have him right in front of us now, so I think this is the only chance we might have to get our money back. We have gone through too much over the past twenty-four hours not to try. Meeting him here so randomly must be more than just a coincidence. Perhaps we were destined to meet him here."

"But how are we going to do this?" he questions.

I sit and begin to think hard about it. I do not feel it is appropriate to make a scene like yesterday, especially with this place being so close to our motel. I somehow need to get Marco out of here so I can interrogate him freely. But on the other hand, I kind of want to see who he is waiting for. Could he be meeting up with Sergio? I figured that they already would have met up at some point over the last day, but perhaps I am wrong. Who else could he be waiting on?

"Let's wait here for the time being," I instruct Teddy. "It looks like he is waiting for someone. Let's see who it is."

"Okay," Teddy agrees.

We wait for some time, but as anxious as we are, Marco appears even more so. Though our sight on him is not entirely perfect due to lighting differences between the inside of the store and outside, his uneasiness is very apparent. He paces through the store, repeatedly checks his phone, and peers out the window. Nervousness exudes from him.

"Which car do you think is his?" I ask Teddy.

"I really don't know," he answers, looking at all four cars parked around the building. "Who knows which one he switched out after yesterday."

"Hmmm… I wonder," I say.

Six minutes pass before Marco picks up his phone to make a call.

"You don't think he has seen us, do you?" Teddy asks.

"I don't think so, but I am not entirely sure," I say. "We are pretty far away right now so he would have to study us hard through the window before making out who we are. I am not sure if he saw me get out of the car earlier, though."

Marco looks at his phone again a short moment after making the call. He must have had bad service or the number he called went straight to voicemail. He anxiously begins scanning the vehicles in the parking lot through the glass.

"Shit!" I say, grabbing onto Teddy's shoulder to pull him down. "Duck down! He'll see us."

We both pull our heads down as not to expose our faces and crouch as much as our bodies will physically allow.

"I think I've decided what I'm going to do," I say to the huddled Teddy.

"What would that be?" he apprehensively asks.

"When he decides to leave, which he probably will do here shortly after being stood up, I'm going to attempt to sneak up on him from behind his car."

Teddy's face sours at the thought.

"I will get into the car with him and interrogate him. He'll listen closely to me when I show him this." I open up my jacket to display the weapon at my side.

"No!" Teddy interjects. "It would be smarter just to tail him with our vehicle and find out where he is going. He could lead us directly to Sergio and the money."

"We can't do that," I disagree. "We cannot, under any circumstance, turn this into another car chase. He will notice at some point, you know. Tailing somebody, especially a suspicious person like Marco right now, is a lot harder than you might think. Plus, there aren't many cars out today. It will be very apparent to him that he is being followed."

I shimmy my head up to see what Marco is doing and realize that he is not inside the building anymore. He has turned to his left and approaches an old, white Ford Explorer.

"He's heading to his car right now. I need to go."

"No," Teddy says, "You…"

"We have to do this my way," I cut him off while opening my door. "Sorry. Don't attempt to interfere. I am gonna take care of this. Hold onto your phone, and I'll hit you up afterward."

Teddy attempts to say something to stop me, but I shut my door before he has the chance.

I shrink down behind the hood of our car to make sure that I am covered from view should Marco glance over in my direction. Marco puts the key into the door to unlock it. I need to make my move quickly.

I stand up and start walking in the Explorer's direction. I approach it from the back-left corner from approximately sixty feet away.

"Please don't turn around," I mutter to myself as I near the unnoticing Marco who swings his door open and sits down in his vehicle. I hold my breath as I get closer because it makes me feel stealthy. This is the longest sixty feet I have ever walked.

Okay, almost there. Just a few more steps until I can get to his window. I drop my right hand to my side and grasp the butt of my gun.

With a couple more feet to go, Marco suddenly turns his head and looks over at me. A look of bewilderment quickly turns to that of horror. He is too late to act, though, as I show him my weapon underneath the left flap of my jacket so only he can see it. His eyes shoot open and his mouth drops, giving me the "Oh my God" look.

I have grasped control of the situation, and Marco knows that it would be stupid to try something foolish now. Everything that has turned out right for the Celettas thus far has quickly shifted, and it is now our turn. Time for me to make the most out of this situation and retrieve what both Teddy and I deserve from this dumbstruck Marco. Their choice of deceit has now come full circle and karma is not on their side.

I make my way to his window, crouch down, and bang my weapon against it twice, producing a *clunk clunk* sound.

"Don't drive away!" I yell through the glass. "I'm going to come around and join you in the passenger's seat."

While holding the gun under my jacket to keep it hidden from civilians, I work my way around the front of the vehicle. Marco does not follow me with his eyes as I walk around but instead slumps over, puts his head to the wheel, and mutters something under his breath. Before swinging the door open to enter, I check to see if anyone has noticed anything abnormal about my approach to the Explorer. From what I can tell, the few people around seem oblivious to us. Everyone minds their own business and is busy with thoughts of holiday cheer in their heads. I look over at Teddy and send a quick nod to let him know that I am alright. I open the door and sit down, immediately pulling out my weapon from beneath my jacket and direct it toward Marco.

Not even a split-second passes before Marco blurts out, "I'm so sorry. You have to listen to me!"

"No!" I retaliate angrily. "You listen to me!"

I am going to be the one in control of this reunion. Marco has already caused enough trouble for me and is no friend of mine. He does not deserve to be treated fairly.

His face is filled with worry as his hands shake on the wheel. He is not prepared to be in this position. Completely caught off guard from my approach, my mere presence shocked him.

"You've made life extremely difficult for me recently, but you didn't think I was smart enough to come back from your brother's little stunt on me," I boldly express. "Well, here I am in the flesh, and free from the prison sentence you hoped I would get. I want my money back for the pain that you have caused me."

"We.. we.. we can make a deal with you," Marco stutters. "You know us, Kev. I will get you what you need."

I become enraged. "How am I supposed to know? Goddamn it! You guys just turned on me like that, after all those years together as friends! How could you do that to me? For all the pain that you've put me through, I am gonna make sure that you don't get any of the cut. That money is mine now! You don't deserve any of it."

The hopeless Marco sighs and shakes his head. "I'm sorry! You don't know how much I regret what has happened and need to explain myself."

"I don't care!" I shoot back. "For this whole time I've known you, not one time did you not have my back. I can never trust you again! You aren't a friend of mine anymore."

"Okay," Marco surrenders. "What can I do to make this right for you?"

He is willing to follow my moves. Marco had no time to plan for my arrival or confrontation. In his position, he really has no other choice but to listen to my demands. Recovering the money should not be difficult now that I have him cornered. After a rough sequence of events, it looks like things might start falling into place now.

"I don't want to make a scene here," I tell him. "I want you to drive out of this gas station. Take a left out on the street and keep going on that road. I want you to keep driving, and I'll give you more directions as we go."

Marco starts up the car, beginning to follow my initial instructions.

I need to get Marco and myself out of this gas station and away from people. I have no idea what lies ahead of us, but the further we are away from the motel, the better. I need to find a quieter place, one with no people so I can discuss the next moves of meeting up with Sergio and getting back the money.

A surrendered Marco pulls out onto the main road. His current state of powerlessness leaves him uneasy. He continually turns his body uncomfortably in the seat. The muscles in his face are tight, as he must be tensing them up to cope with some of the current stress.

Time to think, time to think. I need to question him about Sergio's location. When I get Marco to lead me to Sergio and the money, I will call up Teddy and update him on where I am going to be. Retrieving the money should not be too hard. Any threat of death to Marco will cause Sergio to concede immediately. He will be in a challenging position but will not allow his brother to be harmed. If all goes smoothly, it is possible to retrieve all the money and never need to see the Celetta brothers again in my life. Teddy and I could then channel all of our thoughts and energies into dealing with this post-bank undercover lifestyle. This could actually be that easy.

We are now entering a section of road with groves of trees along both sides. Nothing but frozen wilderness. Though it is lighter than it has been in several days, the dark, creepily long branches along the road hide much of it, leaving nothing but gloomy shadows all around. We have not been driving too far just yet, but it does not bother me. Because it is so quiet and secluded here, I might as well do my interrogating now.

"I want you to pull off the side of the road up there, Marco," I direct him. "Drive right into that little clearing."

A path had been formed from the road into the woods. It looks as though it had been made as some sort of trail. This path will lead me to an ideal spot to have my little talk with Marco.

As I instruct him to do, Marco pulls off onto the path.

"Move farther in!" I say to him.

Being out of sight from all travelers along the road will give us the privacy that being deep in the woods can provide.

Marco drives to a spot where I am satisfied, and I let him know that it is okay to stop. He puts the vehicle in park, and I take a look behind us to see how far away we are from the road. Nothing surrounds us but dormant nature. It is significantly darker here. Perhaps it is not only the trees causing this change in brightness but that of the short day's dusk descending upon us. We are alone.

"Okay," I tell him, "I am going to be respectful first. This thing will go smoothly if you just follow my directions and answer questions appropriately."

Marco nods, not saying a word.

I raise my gun from its lowered position to make a point. I shift my weight in the seat toward him to help steady my aim.

"But if you are not willing to play ball, I will make sure that things get messy," I continue. "I'll say it again. I am not your friend anymore, so don't think that you will receive any compassion from me. I have been through far too much and am sick and tired now."

Marco's blank face stares out the window in front of us.

I begin with my first and most vital question: "Where is Sergio?"

Marco is quiet and continues looking ahead. I give him a moment to gather his thoughts and words, but he never answers.

"Excuse me, Marco?" I emphasize each word, starting to become a little aggravated after he ignores the threat I just made.

A few seconds pass, and he takes a deep breath and slumps down to relax a little.

"I'm sorry, Kev," he says, "but I can't tell you that."

My calmness disappears immediately. I feel the rage build up in my chest and mounts to explode out of my limbs.

"What the fuck do you mean, 'I can't tell you that!?'" I yell.

"I can't tell you," he repeats. "I am not going to put my brother's life in the path of your destruction. I don't trust that you won't kill both him and me."

"Oh! You can be certain that you will indeed die if you don't tell me where he is," I promise him.

Marco finally turns and looks at me, right into my eyes. Newfound confidence emboldens him.

"I don't care if you kill me here. I know you will. You are a murderer at heart. I will gladly sacrifice my own life here to ensure my brother is safe. So go ahead, do it! I'm not saying anything."

I leap at him, grasping his collar with my fist. I yank it across the armrest and shove my gun to his temple. I press the barrel hard into his head and scream right into his face.

"Be smart, Marco!" I holler at him. "Just fucking tell me!"

"No!" he repeats, sternly looking me in the face.

I kneel up in the seat and begin to sweat. The rush of emotion and adrenaline fires up my arms. My finger tightly clenches around the trigger, and I pull him even closer to my face. All the frustration and lack of control of the situation unravels my focus.

"Tell me!" I shout, feeling the vein in my forehead pulsate as I do so.

"No!" he confirms again as he glares back at me through my soul.

The Bad Guy

I muscle down the trigger with all my force as the weapon discharges.

CHAPTER 13

All the intensity and rage of the moment disappears. My heart sinks and my lungs catch up into my throat. Weakness crashes upon me. The heavy gun causes my arm to loosely dangle as it bounces off the center armrest and lands awkwardly into my lap. What have I done?

Marco's body lies in the corner between the driver's door and seat. His eyes do not stare into mine, but instead, focus at an upward angle. He seems to be studying a spot on the ceiling as if his body is ignoring the event that just took place.

Blood is splayed throughout the car. Streams pour from the right side of his face. A mixture of brain and gore specks are dispersed everywhere. I feel the slight moisture of it on my face. The car is covered with this dark red explosion, except for the brighter red splotches on the window that are lightened by the snow reflected through it.

Marco is gone. Taken away just like that in a blink of an eye. The person I have known, cracked jokes, and played board games with is merely a memory now. I always thought that the four of us would grow old with each other. I never believed that the frailty of the human condition would separate us. The weapon in my loose arm only aided in cutting a friend's life short. This was my doing.

Reality has set in. I have become what I hate. I am not merely the bank robber or "criminal" I agreed to live with. I am more than that. I am the taker of lives. I am indeed a cold-blooded killer.

Marco did not deserve an ending like this. No act that he ever did justifies this brutality. I know he may have turned his back on me, but he left me as a full being. I cut his life short. I alone am the reason for this. I stripped him of his existence just like the other lives I have recklessly stolen away.

I feel the blue eyes of the blonde woman staring through me again. The eyes of innocence that penetrate through my lies and can see my real character.

A headache begins to form and my stomach starts to quiver. I throw open the passenger door and launch into the woods to vomit. I plop down on my weak knees and empty my innards next to a tree. When I finish, I begin to shake uncontrollably. My body develops a fever-like chill. I curl my body up against the tree in an attempt to get warm and keep myself together.

I somehow lost my way over the last few years. Though I always felt sick and regretful of my murders, I never believed that I was a killer at heart. I feel the wetness of tears build and blur my vision. I was not able to say goodbye. Neither did Teddy, nor his best friend and brother, Sergio. I feel the tear fall from my left cheek and disappear into the white ground below.

I can still see the smiling face of an exuberant young Marco. He loved life so dearly and took every chance to laugh and enjoy the world around him. He was happy to be surrounded by friends. Now he sits in the white Explorer, alone in his hidden, frozen grave.

If only the police were able to capture me before I regained consciousness yesterday. Marco would be spared, and nobody else would be affected by this monster that I have become. I should not be here. I should not have become this person. I now realize that I lost myself years ago.

Why did I pull the trigger? I really did not want to. Marco was one of my best friends. In the heat of the moment, just like my previous murders, I just broke. I resorted to the barbaric instincts of cavemen. My anger flooded my intellect and took over. I am a fool to believe in my strong intuition and judgment. I am nothing but the common impulse killer I always loathed. I am a hypocrite. I always attempted to hide or explain myself away from that fact, but there is no hiding from it now.

Although I did not back down from my promise, I executed a defenseless friend. The only reason Marco kept his mouth shut was to protect his brother. And now I sit here with his blood on me. He, the blonde girl, and all the other lives that I have taken did not do anything wrong. It was I, and only I that had a choice. I just perpetually chose the wrong one, the one that defines who I am.

I inch my head up from its ducked position between my arms. The chills continue to resonate deep within, but I force myself to look at the vehicle despite the hurt. I will not get back in the car. I cannot do it. Marco needs to be left in peace now and my being anywhere near him will cause disruption to it. I cannot even bear to look at him. Despite every logical reason to clean up the mess or remove any evidence, there is no running away from the guilt. The damage has already been done. I cannot hide from these sins anymore. Consequences for my actions will be deserved.

The shadows from the trees are growing longer and darker by the minute. Though the initial intensity of my fever-like symptoms has passed, that chill still resides within me. I need to get out of here. If I do not die from guilt-ridden grief, the rapidly dropping temperature will certainly get me. The days are short, so it will be dark soon. The darkness will only make the climate worsen.

I put pressure on my knees to stand. I lean into the tree for stability as my legs buckle. I keep my arms folded over my chest and hunch my back to reduce any amount of unnecessary heat loss.

The black, naked branches tower over me, making it difficult to see. The slivers of the sky that I do catch beyond the frightful arms are solid gray. The dreary setting corresponds with the overall state of morbid bleakness.

I have to get out of here. I need to get back to Teddy and the motel. It is a few miles up the road. If I start walking now, I will get back before the temperature freezes me to death. I must walk alongside the street but inside the brush deep enough so nobody sees me. I hope that my weak and suffering body finds the strength to go the distance.

I lift my head one more time to look over at the Explorer. Its bright white appearance contrasts with the dimming daylight and is intimidating to me. I try to avoid looking through the windows so that I will not catch sight of the damage I inflicted. I am scared to see the destruction that my actions have caused. With a last glance at the vehicle, I then lower my head toward my body and turn around. I stumble on the first step to begin my long journey through the endless forest.

CHAPTER 14

I feebly push my body against our motel room door and finally reach the long-awaited warmth. The trek through the woods felt significantly longer than the few miles that it actually was. The chill constantly nagged and bit at me during the journey, and it took the majority of my capacity to grind through it. The physical exertion of the trip is finally over. At last, I can take a breather, sit down, and relax in the comfort of the heated room. There will still be future trouble for me due to the lack of Marco cleanup, but for tonight I will stay put and attempt to find some sort of holiday peace.

As I set foot inside, I see Teddy sitting upright at the far side of the room looking toward me. He jumps at my arrival and quickly grabs the gun next to him on the table.

"Put that gun away!" I call to him. "It's only me, don't be scared."

After an unusually long pause, Teddy decides that it is okay and puts the weapon back on the table. He should not be this skeptical because it is just me. He accepts that he is safe, takes a long breath, and appears to relax some.

He sits behind a long table loaded with several different food options. Closest to me sits another chair with a paper plate and some plastic utensils on the table in front of it. It is not the ideal Christmas dinner, but Teddy must have made the most of what we had in the room. Like I thought, picking up extra food at the gas station would have been unnecessary.

Teddy studies me as I enter and does not move or speak. He just sits there and looks me up and down. He stares at my features and attempts to figure out what happened based on my demeanor. A puzzled expression appears on his face. He scrunches his lower lip and slightly squints his left eye.

My fatigued presence must be throwing him off. How am I going to break the news of Marco's death to him? I did not have the energy to think about it on my way back over here because all of my focus was directed toward staying alive in the bitter cold. I do not know where I should start. Should I explain my story and then break the terrible news, or just tell it to him straight? I am not sure how you tell someone that you just murdered a friend with whom they spent their entire life.

"What happened?" an anxious Teddy finally speaks. "I've been sitting here for a long time without any word or anything from you. You were supposed to call me. I thought that you were killed or captured."

Without waiting for my answer, Teddy stands and picks up a heavy blue blanket on the bedside to bring over to my shivering body.

"You are going to get hypothermia if you aren't kept wa..." He stops midway to me.

He peers down and sees some of the blood that splattered over my clothing.

He then looks up into my eyes and stutters, "You.. you.. you killed him, didn't you?"

My thoughts that were struggling to find the words to break the news to him suddenly ceased. There is no breaking it to him now. He knows what does not need to be said.

I do not say a word, but instead, gently nod my head to affirm the truth.

The revelation strikes him down. He drops the blanket on the floor, takes a few steps back, and falls into his seat. He stares blankly toward the back wall, obviously dumbstruck by the information.

My body begins to thaw due to the toasty temperature of the room. I pull out the chair across from Teddy and sit myself down, ignoring the blanket that he just dropped. There is not much I can say to him now. No words of assurance or defense on my behalf would be appropriate. Teddy just needs to get over this initial shock and understand what has happened. I will explain everything that needs to be said once he is settled and can find the words to speak.

I help myself to the meal that Teddy has laid out. I start with some mashed potatoes that had been microwaved out of a box. He did a great job of putting together a respectable Christmas meal considering the limited choices. We have mashed potatoes, heated slices of deli ham, canned green beans and corn, and some warm rolls soaked with the right amount of garlic and butter. I have not eaten anything all day. I do not know if my lack of hunger has been caused by the emotion of my evil act or the miserable weather, but I have not even thought about food until now.

I look up to the still speechless Teddy preoccupied with his thoughts. He stares blankly at the center part of his plate. Whether it be from revisiting old times he had with Marco or the realization that he is not coming back, Teddy's mind is working hard thinking about something.

Poor guy. His life is not what it should be. Pure excitement and riches are what I promised him when he vowed to take on this life of lawbreaking. I did not need to persuade him, though, as the only thing he wanted to do was whatever we were doing.

He loved the Celetta brothers and me. He has been one loyal brother to me his entire life. It was wrong of me to do this to him. Pain, suffering, and insecurity are the only things that I have delivered to him. He could have been great at many other things and could have been a productive and generous individual in this world. He was always a good student. He could have grown up to be a doctor, a successful businessman, or anything for that matter, instead of stealing from society with the three of us.

"How did it happen?" Teddy finally speaks, with his attention on me again.

His deep brown eyes focus on me, attentive to hear the words of a killer.

"Well..." I say, trying to figure out how to start. "Everything just sort of seems like a blur. We drove down the road a couple of miles and I led him to a trail where no one could see us. I really wanted to figure out Sergio's location so we could find the money. He was unrelenting against my threats and unwilling to tell me. I tried to get it out of him, but he was not breaking. He did not trust me. He thought I would go kill Sergio if he told me."

I stop for a moment during the explanation. I cannot pinpoint the direct cause, the exact tipping point that made me pull the trigger. I usually react intellectually instead of emotionally, but this one got away from me. I killed Marco out of pure anger, period.

I continue my recollection with honesty. "I just killed him. I got angry and frustrated, and the only power I had was with the weapon I had in my hand. With the escalation in my fury, I snapped, and that was it. I can't believe it's over. And just like that, he is gone."

That was all that needed to be said. I was not in a position where I valiantly fought for my life against his overwhelming brutality. No accidental misfire that cost him his life either. I executed him out of anger.

The amber shading in Teddy's iris seems to have darkened after hearing this. I killed something within him. My murder of Marco was not the only thing that caused this. Over the last few years, I have subjected Teddy to pain and misery, and the death of Marco must have finally taken its toll.

My tear ducts want to open, but the physical fatigue and exhaustion prevent any flow of emotion. I not only killed Marco today, but I also killed Teddy's spirit. I want all of this to go away. I want to take back the pull of the trigger, the anger, the bank job, and, most of all, the initial idea that a life of delinquency was the way to go.

"I'm sorry," I shoot out to Teddy. "I'm so sorry. I wish I never did it."

Teddy, still speechless, continues just to sit there, wondering what to think. His eyes draw away from mine and back onto the plate that he set for himself. I acknowledge the crushing sadness in his demeanor and lower my head to my own plate and stare blankly into my potatoes.

Where do I go from here? How does one come back from all the pain and anxiety that they cause? It is too late for me. There is nothing I can do but just sit here, staring down into my plate and not cause any more harm.

I suddenly think about his brother. Poor Sergio. He must be deeply troubled tonight, waiting for the brother that will never return. How unfortunate that this would occur on the most joyful of holidays. No emotional torment exceeds that of losing the life of a loved one. Sergio will wait in fear and agony, awaiting the arrival of a sibling that he will never see again. It does not matter what he has done to me. His actions are negligible compared to mine. I have gone too far, and my actions are unforgivable.

While looking down into my plate, I catch my own bloody shirt in my peripherals. My stomach tightens due to the view of both food and gore together. There is no way I can swallow an ounce more of this food without getting this dreadful killer's apparel off of me. Everything about this makes me sick. I get up and immediately rip off the garment speckled with death and place it into a plastic grocery bag I find in a gym bag of supplies next to my bed. I do not wish to put on another shirt, so I wrap myself in a large towel. Though the spray only hit the outer clothing I was wearing, I still feel dirty and do not want to tarnish any more clothes with the invisible grossness that envelopes me. I return to the seat across from Teddy and drop myself into it again.

Teddy gazes up at me and instantly comes out from his zone of thoughts. "So what did you do with his body?" he almost seems to demand.

Taken aback by such an unexpected question, I realize that he has put his emotions aside for the moment to be intelligent and understand the details following the murder. He is looking for any missteps that can potentially get us into trouble if identified. Unfortunately, I reacted with emotion and did not thoroughly contemplate the consequences of my actions.

"I left him there in the white Explorer. I made him pull off into a small clearing a few miles down the road. Right down the trail that I mentioned earlier. That is where he still is," I say.

"That's it?" Teddy shoots at me. "You just left him there only a few miles from this place? I thought that you were smart and careful. He will be found, and when he is, they will definitely be looking around this area. We are right fucking here, Kev! Everything we have done to this point will not matter after such a stupid move like that."

Teddy was sharp and is visibly angry with me. Anger that I have never seen in him before. I have taught him to be methodical in his actions and leave as little to chance as possible. I would never have allowed such a blatant lack of regard in the past. The truth is that I just do not care anymore. I am not concerned with having to face the consequences of my sins. I am done hiding from who I really am.

"I'm sorry Teddy," I say with sincerity. "I really can't hide it. I'm done with running from my actions. I guess if they find me, I'll deserve it. I think I may even feel better if I am punished for all of the crimes that I've committed."

"What about me?" the agitated Teddy continues. "You may be fine with all of this, but what about me? You were supposed to look out for me. You were the one who promised to help me out no matter what. I'm not ready to go down just because 'you don't care anymore.' I know this is a tough time for you now, but pull yourself together, Kevin. Be smart!"

He unloads his mixture of worry and annoyance on me. I am not sure if it is his reaction to the shock that I murdered Marco, or his actual fear of being caught, but his blunt response really surprises me. Perhaps I should have considered Teddy before I left that clearing. Maybe I need to set all this straight just for his sake and not necessarily mine.

"Let me think about this, Teddy." I begin to try to set this right. "We aren't in bad shape now, so this can still be fixed. Let's take this one step at a time, and I will make this right. I really do apologize for getting you into this. You know that I will always look after you and make sure you're alright, ahead of whatever I am thinking about myself at the moment."

Though Teddy is still frowning, he seems to have cooled off some. He gives an understanding nod and knows that I will do the best I can to help him.

"You at least grabbed his cell phone then, right?" Teddy asks.

"Cell phone?" I question.

"Goddamn it!" Teddy shakes his head. "You remember seeing him call someone at the gas station? He definitely had it on him. If you weren't so blinded by anger, you could've used it to see if he'd been talking to Sergio. If so, you could have used it to call Sergio directly and threatened to harm Marco unless he told you his location. That phone could have been the one thing that would've gotten us to Sergio."

I never considered that idea until he mentioned it. I let my emotions get the best of me and allowed my common sense to slip away. I would have gotten to Sergio somehow or some way if I had just concentrated on it. The rage of my vengeance overtook my logic. There was a way for me to make everything work, I just blatantly chose not to accept it.

"Don't worry," I assure him. "Not much time has passed since the incident. I'll go out later, clean up, and take care of everything else that needs to be done."

Even though my words to Teddy sound reassuring, I feel terrified to have to go back to the Explorer and see the lifeless Marco lying there in the middle of that clearing. I do not think I could consciously get myself to face him. Even the thought of the dark, bitter night surrounding his vehicular tomb gives me the shivers.

"Let's eat now, then," Teddy says, putting aside his worry for the moment. "We'll go back and take care of it afterward. I just want to try to enjoy this meal and be able to eat in peace."

Following his words, the room goes quiet except for the sounds of the slicing of his knife against the ham and the subtle chewing of food. Even though the recent queasiness from the sight of blood hampered my hunger, I force a bite of green beans that spurs my appetite.

With the persistent tension over the past day and a half, I finally feel a slight sense of peace with the warmth and quietness around this mediocre, yet satisfying meal. I sit here with my best friend, comfortably eating with a momentary loss of sorrow. I wish I could live the rest of my life like this moment, away from all fear and tribulation. I want to laugh and joke at the dinner table with my friends and family, surrounded by their smiles and cheerful faces. That is all I want and nothing more. I do not want the money, planning, exhilaration, and worry. I used to think that is what I wanted, but I was incorrect. No happiness can come from living so dishonestly. I want to be good, I want to be humble, I want both peace and contentment. I took a wrong turn and ended up somewhere nobody wants to be.

How do I change from here? Over the last few years, I have been blind to my own rapidly disintegrating morals. Instead of consciously understanding that my actions have been wrongful, I have rationalized and adjusted my morals to a point way beyond an acceptable standard. I steal, rob, murder, and create chaos, yet still justify to myself a reason for doing all of them. I never grew up with the intention of doing all of the appalling things that I have done. Time and poor decision-making got me to this point. It started with a slight relaxation of my morals, but I kept loosening them until they spiraled out of control. If I had a chance to go back and talk to my former self, he would be incredibly disappointed with how I have turned out today. I am the person that, as a child, I used to loathe. I became the bad guy, far from the hero that every child wants to be.

I am no Edmond Dantes. If vengeance is ever justifiable, mine is definitely not. I am just a villain trying to come out on top. I was so irritated at the Celetta brothers for what they did to me, yet there really is no justice served by one bad guy taking revenge on another. There are no heroes amongst thieves. Who cares if they wronged me by setting me up to go to jail? I deserve much worse. I take the lives from those around me. I have subjected my friends to psychologically intense situations as a result of my murders. These friends have had to reluctantly stay alongside me through all of the dreadful things that I have done.

I do not feel the villainous type, though. I have always thought that those who were evil understood that they were so and just chose to be so. Time and time again in literature and movies, the antagonists clearly know that they are indeed immoral and use any means necessary to get what they want. They inherently recognize the hero in their story. The only struggles they encounter are those involving the obstacles they face in their confrontations with the protagonist. They never think about or are conflicted by the thoughts of regret or remorse. They are only frustrated by things that get in the way of their own wants and needs.

I never thought that one could be evil and also feel the negative sensation of doing wrong. Most villains do not consider themselves "bad" but instead adjust their definitions of morals to a laxer state to compensate. As I mentioned before, this is what happened to me. I have not been cognizant of my true nature due to my internal arguments of being a "good" person. I have accepted these new arguments in my favor to stay oblivious to the actual person I have become.

I do not want to be this person. For years I have battled my own feelings, and until recently, never quite understood my own character. I do not deserve the money. Sergio can keep it. What is critical for me now is that I recognize and follow who I want to be. That alone should be my only goal right now.

I look up after dwelling in my thoughts for that short while. Teddy continues to work on the food, grabbing more potatoes from the microwaved plastic container between us. I have done my fair share of work on the meal as well. It has been quite some time since I have sat down and eaten something this substantial.

"Teddy?" I ask, trying to get his attention from the long silence between us.

"Yeah?" He glances up at me, looking like he has just been pulled out of some zone of deep concentration.

I decide that instead of working him into a discussion, I will just ask him directly. "Am I a bad person?" I ask.

Teddy blinks a few times, understandably being unprepared for such a question.

"No, you're not a bad person," he says. "You care for people. Look at what you've done for me. You've had my back for as long as I can remember. Look at what you did yesterday, saving me from the police. If you were really that 'bad,' you would've left me in that car."

"But what about my lifestyle?" I ask. "Think about what I do for a living. My profession is that of a thief or criminal, stealing not out of necessity, but out of choice."

Teddy sort of shrugs. "I dunno," he answers. "Is it really that bad? I know it's against the law, but we aren't making this personal. We are just doing what we need to do to survive. You know, make a living of some sort."

"Now how about my killing of people? No good person would ever resort to such an extreme. Hell, most of the people that I've murdered never needed to be."

"What's with all these questions?" Teddy starts getting frustrated. "Goddamn! This probably isn't the best time for a self-evaluation, Kev. I am not really in that mindset now. You have always taught me to be smart and think about the situation at hand. We have a dead body with direct traces to us not far from where we are now. Let's just finish this dinner, take care of everything out there, and then you can talk with me about your self-assessment."

The flustered Teddy goes back to his meal without answering my question. I do not blame him for doing so, as it has been a long couple of days for both of us. He is typically receptive and understanding when I need his help, but the stress has taken a toll on him.

However, my interest in this matter has been bothering me so much that I have to get this off my chest now. It has been such a burden recently, and I really need to find out who I am.

"Teddy," I say, hoping to have his assistance with this second try. "I'm sorry to keep bugging you about this, but I really need to figure out who I am now. I need this serious talk so that I don't lose myself. I don't want to ask a lot from you, but can you please answer these questions to help me?"

He puts down his fork and studies me with a new appreciation for my internal struggle. His upset demeanor changes immediately to one of understanding. Even in the worst of times, Teddy can put aside his emotions and listen to me. That is one reason why he has always been a great friend of mine.

"Okay," he says. "You aren't a bad guy, Kev. I mean, you've killed guys before, but sometimes in order to get what you need, you have to act and make quick decisions. Sergio, Marco, and I have never had what it takes to make a move like that. Without you, we wouldn't have been able to get away with or do the things that we have done. We've been put in situations, and that is the way that you responded. You don't kill out of hate or anger. You do it because you think it is the right thing to do at the moment."

"I've murdered Marco, though. No good person would have ever done that."

"Well, the Celettas messed up and understood the consequences. After doing something like that to a friend, stabbing you in the back and all, it would be crazy not to expect some sort of retaliation if their plan didn't work out. Unfortunately for them, their idea didn't quite work out as planned. You see, vengeance is part of human nature. Again, you've been placed in these situations and you responded the only way that you could. Even the fact that this is bothering you so much makes you a good person. No bad person would deeply contemplate the things that you do."

"Thank you, Teddy. That really means a lot to me. That is exactly what I needed." I lie.

I nod to him, and he smiles at his ability to help a friend. He then returns to finish up the last bit of his meal.

Though he is being sincere, something did not quite fit. It sounded like a lot of the same excuses that I used to feed him over the years. Though I never really talked to the group about the murders, when I did talk about them, I used much of the same phrases and explanations that Teddy just did. Receiving those responses from Teddy did not give me the comfort that I had hoped for. I do not know if he agrees with those theories or not, or just regurgitated them in an attempt to make me feel better.

It is a good thing that Teddy will never have to feel the way that I do. He is no killer and understands and respects human life just as he did as a young child. That is one thing that I can pride myself on. Even with all the awful things that I have done, I have never moved Teddy to the same murderous mindset as me. Instead, I have steered him away from it.

It will take some time to really comprehend who I am as a person and re-evaluate myself. As long as I maintain a positive mindset, I hope to stay away from these acts that would identify me as a "bad guy."

The Bad Guy

CHAPTER 15

I recall the details of the incident as though it just took place moments ago. That day still haunts me and reoccurs in my nightmares. It was the start of something terrible, a moment I could not take back. As much as it resonates with me, I continue to act in a counter-productive manner spurred on by this event. There is no reason I should keep doing what I do. My destructive behavior is a direct result of what happened that day.

It happened four years ago, right at the tail end of summer. Sergio, Marco, Teddy, and I were captivated by the lifestyle that we had recently embraced. It was an exciting time where our deviant behavior coincided with our youthful recklessness. At that time, the robberies were not committed as our source of income but were merely an experiment. They were a way to create memorable experiences that the four of us could share together.

Knocking over banks was out of the question back then. That was too above our heads and too risky. We would not have even considered it anyway. All we did was knock over a few small stores and gas stations on the outskirts of town where traffic flow and amount of associated risk was limited. The payout from these places was nothing spectacular, but the rush that we received from robbing them was immense.

Despite what some people may tell you, small jobs are relatively easy to get away with. All we really needed to do was to wear masks, ensure that not too many people were around, pre-plan parking to avoid the security cameras, have a fake license plate, and move fast enough to get out of there. Of course, at times we set off alarms, but we were in and out of there so quick that escaping was no big issue. We had an escape plan where we would switch out cars shortly after leaving. The police would then be searching for the wrong vehicle. We usually tied up the employees and customers so that they were physically unable to call for help immediately after our escape. There are a few more aspects that we took into account based on what our specific situation was, but I do not wish to drone on with the particulars of each unique case.

With the continued string of robberies, it is just a matter of time before one slips up and gets caught. We just happened to be extremely lucky and did not mess up badly enough to be captured. Our continued freedom gave us a false sense of invincibility which kept us coming back for more.

On this particular day, we intended to rob a small gas station in a nearby town. It was an older station with only a few semi-antique pumps. The location was not strategically placed to maximize traffic flow and was far from the nearest highway. I rarely saw any customers there. Perhaps at some point in time, it had been used and visited more often. However, years relocation of commercial and residential zones left this little store surrounded by miles of thick forest and secluded in the corner of a T-intersection.

This business was on its last legs and probably should have closed up shop ages before. Looking back, it was not worth the risk to rob a store that at most held maybe a few hundred dollars at one time. Knocking over a struggling establishment was not only unethical but was also just a nasty thing to do.

Being naive, though, the comprehension of what we were actually doing went right over our heads. I was too intrigued by our devious behavior to recognize the repercussions of our actions.

Behind the pumps was a small building that required individuals to go inside to prepay for their fuel. The pumps themselves were not modern enough to take credit cards, so it was necessary to go inside to pay. As in most convenience stores/gas stations, a single cashier stood behind the counter accepting payments for gas, snack, and beverage purchases. The size of the building was not very large, perhaps 400 square feet or less. It appeared to be about the size of a standard hotel room.

On the day that we decided to commit our crime, it was still considerably warm outside. The intensity of the sun and summer enthusiasm were noticeably on the decline. People were settling down after the vacation season and getting ready for school to begin.

We all rode together in the same car. Sergio was driving, I was in the passenger seat, and both Marco and Teddy were riding in the back. The plan was simple. Because the gas station was located at the corner of a T-intersection, Sergio would drive on the road behind the building. The purpose of coming from this direction was to avoid the security camera on the front of the building pointed at the intersection. He would take a U-turn before reaching the station and park on the side of the road so that when we escaped, we would never come into the camera's view. We would hop out and approach the building from behind. Our counterfeit license plate would be discarded afterward in case anyone witnessed our getaway.

Sergio finished the U-turn and pulled up to the side of the road.

"You all ready?" I asked, looking around the car to make sure that everyone had their ski masks, gloves, and pistols in hand.

The handguns were an accessory we had all recently acquired. We figured that most people would take us seriously if we held such an intimidating weapon. We specifically discussed not using them for what they were designed to do, but instead use them as a catalyst for fear. People are more apt to acquiesce to the demands of those brandishing weapons than even slightly consider the idea of resistance. We were less likely to find ourselves in dangerous confrontations and able to take complete control of a situation with time limitations. We all agreed that the benefits of carrying the pistols outweighed any negatives. We knew the purpose of them and would never, under any circumstance, need to or intend to discharge the weapons.

We understood that what we were doing was looked down upon, but we felt the moral consequences were insignificant in the entire scheme of our lives. Because we were not inherently "evil" people, we did have our boundaries. Murder was not even a consideration. We all knew that performing such an act would automatically corrupt a clean conscience and put us outside the realm of innocence and into that of wickedness. As reckless and irrational as we were at the time, not one of us was willing to bear such a blatant mark of badness.

With everyone's nod of approval signifying readiness, I addressed them one last time. "Okay! It looks like we are not gonna have too much trouble in there today 'cause it doesn't look too busy from what I can tell. Let's get in there, make sure the room is clear, and have Sergio and Teddy take care of collecting the money up front. Ready? Let's go!"

Following that delivery, all four of us thrust open the car doors almost simultaneously and jumped out onto the road. We hurriedly made our way to the backside of the building which had no windows that allowed visibility from the inside. We then rounded the left side of the building, which was also windowless. The clerk's counter was on the other side of that wall. Sergio, who was leading the way, stopped for a moment to make sure we were all ready to round the last corner and rush inside as quickly as possible. Upon confirmation that we were all ready, he took off to the front door, threw it open, and the rest of us flowed into the small building. The employee behind the desk jumped at the sight of us, and his eyes widened from the unexpected surprise on the dull routine day.

"Get 'em up!" Sergio shouted at the clerk who did not think twice about doing so.

I ran to the back of the store and peered down the two aisles to see if any customers were hiding behind them. Marco stayed near the front of the building and looked for anybody up there.

"Clear!" I yelled after observing that we were the only ones inside. Marco promptly shouted the same thing.

"Check out the bathroom," Sergio then said as he and Teddy made their way around the counter.

"Let's go!" I signaled to Marco, who followed me as I hurried down the short hallway adjacent to the counter.

There was a small universal bathroom in the back. I remember it being fairly clean when I was scouting this store in the past but just looked dirty from several years of use. The tile, sink, and toilet all looked to be original.

"Stand by me on my left in case something happens," I instructed Marco as I got ready to push open the door. "I doubt there is anyone inside, but be ready just in case."

Both Marco and I put our weapons up in the ready position as I prepared to burst in. I was anxious but knew that the possibility of anyone being inside was slim, so was not overly so. I clasped my hand around the knob and threw the door open.

We both extended our arms and aimed inside. It was dark, but with the limited light from the small hallway, I was instantly able to determine that there were no occupants. Although it was not needed, after a more thorough search we turned around and moved back to the main room. Teddy was waiting for the clerk to open the register so he could gather the small amount of cash while Sergio threatened that scared clerk with his weapon.

"We're good!" I yelled to them. "It is only us in here. You guys about finished up with that so we can get on outta here?"

"Yeah," Sergio said, still watching the clerk. "We'll be finished up in no time. This was quite an easy task."

Sergio was right. This was not a difficult chore at all. It was almost too easy. The adrenaline rush that I usually felt in those situations was not there. Everything was progressing smoothly and the execution was seamless. I wondered at the time if we were getting too good at the small stuff and needed to move up to the next level.

Marco moved to the window up front and stared out into the street as a lookout. I, on the other hand, stayed by the back of the building and watched Teddy and Sergio finish their job behind the counter.

The clerk, who was a middle-aged Indian man, opened the register for Teddy and was noticeably not as comfortable as we were because his arm shook violently as he opened it.

"I don't care," he said to us. "Please take the money and let me be. I don't want any problems."

Because of his reaction, I could tell that we were golden. There were silver flecks throughout the little bit of hair he had left. Behind his glasses, I could see in his small eyes that he was not going to give us any resistance. When he got the register open, Teddy immediately started rummaging through it and placing the few stacks in a small bag he had brought with him.

It only took him a few moments to collect, so he fastened the bag and said, "We're good! Let's go!"

"Alright! Everybody good?" Sergio asked.

"We still need to tie this guy up," I said.

Without answering immediately, Sergio picked up the phone on the desk and flung it to the ground. I could hear a combination of metal and plastic smashing as it hit. He stomped on it a few times more to guarantee its destruction. He lightly frisked the man to make sure no cell phone was on him either.

"He can't call for help anymore," Sergio said. "Now let's get out of here and not waste any more time."

As annoyed as I was for his stupid little scene and unnecessary behavior, starting a fight with him about it would have been a horrible idea. The clerk really could not contact anyone immediately, so I agreed just to leave him and escape. Tying him up would prove to be inefficient, and delay us anyway.

"Fine!" I told him, "Let's get out of here."

With that, Marco, who was right next to the entryway, opened the door. Sergio turned away from the clerk that he was holding hostage and headed toward the door. Teddy scooted by the same clerk to get out from behind the desk to follow Sergio. I began walking from the backside of the building toward the front to tail all three of them out the door.

Everything up to this point was going remarkably well, but I was still bothered by the slight deviation from our initial plan. I was thinking about the getaway as I passed the front desk. From the corner of my eye, I saw a sudden movement.

Time seemed to slow down as I shifted my head and eyes to understand what was going on. It took my mind a few hundredths of a second to comprehend the sight in front of me. Somehow the clerk procured a shotgun and stood there, directing it toward Teddy's back. All three of my friends were moving toward the door facing away from the clerk, so I was the only one able to witness this phenomenon taking place. In that instant, I had to decide what to do next. The fear, mixed with a staunch willingness to protect my friend, overcame any delay of action. It became a race against time as I raised my own firearm. At any moment, the slightest amount of pressure from his finger would be the end of Teddy. His life depended on the quickness of my action.

Without the proper aim, but pointed in the general direction, I got two shots off as I moved my arm upward. I did not see the first bullet, but the second one penetrated the back wall right above the clerk's head and ejected a small amount of drywall from the impact. An ear-popping *BOOM!* erupted from the end of his weapon as the glass shattered from one of the windows up front. As his shotgun discharged, he fell behind the desk and disappeared from view.

All three of my friends jumped at hearing the discharged weapons and immediately jerked around to see what happened. Instead of drawing their firearms, lack of experience caused them to freeze in place and stare at me. The clerk's shotgun round had missed Teddy by a few feet, blasting through the front window to his left. The surprise or possible penetration of my bullet must have thrown his alignment off, allowing Teddy's body to still be in one piece.

Without knowing whether or not I had killed or even hit the clerk, I moved to the side of the counter, kept my weapon in the ready position, and prepared to lunge over it to see what possible damage I had done. With both fear and caution, I thrust my upper body on top of the desk to peer down.

The first thing I recognized was the significant amount of blood, beginning to puddle underneath him. The white shirt he was wearing was quickly turning bright pink and red as it soaked up the liquid. The flow of the darkest fluid emerged periodically from the center of his chest in sync with his breathing. Both of his hands were loosely placed over the spot, shaking from the extensive amount of pain that the wound produced. His shotgun laid on the floor right next to his body but was not an issue or threat given his current condition.

It hit me. I could not believe what I had done. I just shot an innocent man who was only scared and reacted. In that instant, with almost no time or thought at all, I severely wounded another human being. It took no effort to put him into such a weak and critical condition. I, Kevin White, somehow did this to him. I always assumed that people who reacted this way resorted to this kind of behavior because of primal instinct. I never considered myself to be this primeval. The gravity of the situation struck a chord in me as I watched him lay there, struggling to hold onto his gift of life.

Upon seeing my reaction, the other three gathered around the counter to peer down to figure out what happened. As my friends stared at him, I gazed at the stupefied looks on their faces. They had nothing to say, but neither did I as we just looked down at the dying man. Our rush to get out of there was not an issue anymore. Time seemed to freeze as we continued to look down at the destruction.

I knew I could not do anything to help him without jeopardizing all of us, so I decided to do the only thing I could. With everyone stuck in the moment and refusing to take any action, I knew I had to. We had to get out of there and stick to an escape plan.

"Let's get out of here," I finally said.

Without looking at me, they all nodded their heads and agreed with my suggestion. I took one more look down at the tormented man. His eyes were clenched shut as he was straining with all his energy to push back against impending death. Without saying a word, I wished him the best and prayed that he could hold on until someone else could find him there. I made my way to the door where the other three followed me out as I cowardly ran from the mess that I had created.

The trip back was shrouded in complete silence. No one said a single word inside the car, and we barely spoke while hiding out together that night. In fact, even days and years afterward, I have never been asked about the details of the event nor my feelings associated with it. I think that the group has been afraid to talk with me about such a taboo topic as killing, fearing that bringing back the memories would destroy the fake stable façade that I put on for them.

I found out from the news that later that day, another car stopped by to get gas and the driver found the clerk's body inside. By the time the guy had gotten there, though, it was too late. The clerk, by the name of Shivam Jain, had already lost too much blood and perished alone in the building. I cannot describe the amount of sadness that I experienced that night and have felt every night since. Each time I close my eyes I see the tortured man lying there in his puddle of blood, fighting agonizing pain to hold onto life. He died there alone. That image is seared into my memory and is a result of my own action. It haunts me, keeps me up at night, and reoccurs in my nightmares. It has become a part of me that cannot be understood, forgotten, or forgiven.

One would think that with an affliction such as this, my inclination toward murder would be suppressed. Instead, my finger now tends to pull the trigger more easily in confrontational situations. My actions defy logic.

I sweat at night thinking about that poor clerk and the other unfortunate lives that I have personally cut short. I question my choices but continue to go down the same road again and again. It is a drug from which I cannot rehabilitate. Whatever the reason, it has nonetheless made me the wretched man I am today.

The Bad Guy

CHAPTER 16

Bzzzz... Bzzzz... Bzzzz... my phone vibrates atop the side table suddenly, waking me up from a deep sleep.

"Shit!" I yell aloud. I must have dozed off. I took a shower, got dressed, and planned to clean up the Marco mess in the woods. Falling asleep was not supposed to happen.

I reach for the phone. Who the hell is calling me?

I look at the number on the phone and realize that it is Teddy. I take a quick scan of the room and the bed next to mine and become aware that he is not here.

I open the phone and put it to my ear. "Hello?"

"Hey Kev, I gotta tell you something!" Teddy says.

Without missing a beat, I do not let him tell me, but instead begin to apologize. "I'm sorry Teddy, I don't know what I was thinking. I can't believe that I ended up falling asleep at a time like this. I just..."

"Don't worry about that," Teddy cuts me off. "I saw that you were completely out of it, so I decided to leave you sleeping and take care of the cleanup myself. Think of it as my Christmas gift to you. I'm calling you because there is something we need to do right now. You ready to hear about this?"

The excitement in his voice frightens me. He rushes through his speaking with an upbeat tempo, ready to burst with this news.

"I guess so," I brace myself.

"Okay!" Teddy continues. "While I was out here in this little clearing, I pulled the cell phone out of Marco's pocket. After I finished getting rid of all this evidence you left out in the open, I got an idea. Because it was after midnight when I got here, I could tell that Sergio had been worried because of all the missed calls on Marco's phone. The missed calls couldn't have been from anybody else but Sergio. I decided to call him back from it. No special passcode is required for these prepaid phones, so it was no problem calling him back."

"You called him back!?" I exclaim.

"I did!" Teddy affirms. "I called Sergio back from Marco's phone, and he was more than willing to answer to see what had become of his lost brother."

"What did you say?" I ask, incredibly intrigued.

"Calm down, calm down, Kevin," he says, trying to slow me down, obviously loving the fact that I am so interested.

"Well," he says, "I didn't quite tell him that his little brother is dead. What good would that do for us? I told him that you and I have Marco as our hostage and are willing to meet up to negotiate the terms on which we hand him back over. And, as you know, those terms being the money that they unrightfully stole from us yesterday. Fear-stricken Sergio had no other option but to accept this offer that I placed in front of him. I made him give me the address of where he's staying so that you and I can go claim the money that he owes us. Sounds like a hell of a plan, huh?"

Teddy is proud of himself. He believes that he made an intelligent decision from such an unfortunate situation.

"What do you intend we do when Sergio realizes that we don't have his younger brother with us?" I ask.

"I dunno," Teddy responds. "That's what I have you for. I want you to decide what needs to happen here. You're a smart guy. I'm sure you'll be able to shift the situation in our favor. You are always quick on your feet and ready to make the right move."

Though I may still be alive due to my decision-making, I would not consider all of my choices as "the right moves." There really is not an appropriate way to approach Sergio. I cannot face him and tell him that his brother was killed by my own hand. Any confrontation with him now would only result in more destruction. I would not be able to live with myself if I killed or physically harmed Sergio too. I am through with all this vengefulness and greed for money. Nothing positive can come from meeting with him.

Teddy needs to understand that I intend to change myself and become a different person. Perhaps my questions at dinner did not suggest my new mindset well enough. The days of ruining innocent lives and the psychological self-torment I have endured over such acts are behind me now.

"I am done with all this, Teddy," I say. "Sergio has already had enough bad things happen to him in the last day, too. Who cares if he stabbed us in the back and left us for the police? We made it out fine anyway, and we are smart enough to continue moving forward. He lost a brother because of me. Let's just give him a break this time. That is the least he deserves from all the years of friendship."

"You kidding me?" Teddy blurts out. "Don't you want to end this with the upper hand and prove to him that messing with us was the worst decision he has ever made? I don't care if you have to work through your own conflicting morals and stay out of this one. I am going no matter what and will take care of this myself if I need to. I don't need you to come with me. You may feel that you've already done enough to him and anything else would be unjustified, but what about me? I feel like there is still more to be settled on my end. I never killed anyone, I never cheated anyone, I have never done anything to harm anyone whatsoever and still got screwed. You taught me to take a stand for myself and here it is. You cannot talk me out of this. I want to take back what is rightfully mine."

Such a prompt and candid response catches me off guard. I am surprised that he actually feels so strongly about this. This hunger for revenge is something I never saw in his character before. He generally tries to stay away from any conflict around him. I never realized through any of our discussions during the last day and a half or so that Teddy had such strong feelings against the Celetta brothers for doing this to us. To him, this was not just any old conflict, this finally pushed him to the limit of what he could take. Marco and Sergio took this to another level and made it personal for him.

"Nothing that I can say will talk you out of this, will it?" I ask him.

"Don't try, Kev," he answers. "I've had enough of being the one that people can walk over. I'm not merely a stepping-stone for anyone else's ambitions. I need to do this for me this time. I am going to get our money back."

"As much as I really don't want you to do it, I cannot allow you to go over there alone. I need to look after you like I always have. I hope you understand and respect my decision. Sergio can be dangerous, and getting the money from him, especially without Marco, will not be a walk in the park. I need to come with you in case you need any assistance."

"I would not want it any other way," Teddy says. "It means a lot to me, and you having my back is something I don't think I could do without. You've been there for me time and time again, and I admire the brother that you've become. This will probably be the finest hour of our friendship."

Teddy's appreciation of my cooperation gives me a little hope. Perhaps I was wrong about keeping him from going. He will not be going on some mindless, violent rampage to prove what he is worth to Sergio. A peaceful negotiation might give him the closure that he needs with his longtime friend. All of us could then move on and hope to make an honest living in this world. This could be the end of dark days for all of us.

"I'm finished up here and will be back to pick you up with the Civic in a few minutes," Teddy says. "Put on some warm clothes because it is getting extremely cold out."

"Will do, my friend," I say in response. "See ya shortly."

"Later, Kev," he says before ending the call.

I put down the phone and hurry over to one of the dressers. Though the heater is on in our room, it cannot compete with the significantly decreasing outside temperature. I dress into a sweater, pants, jacket, hat, and gloves as fast as I can. I even decide to throw on an extra pair of socks in an attempt to warm up my already freezing feet. I feel that the weather is not going to be kind to us tonight.

As I dress, nervousness begins to build within me. It seems like such a long time since I last saw Sergio. This will be the last time too. I am afraid of his reaction to the news that his brother is dead. I have no idea how he will handle such a situation. Hell, how am I going to handle it? Should I let Teddy do his thing and wait outside? That is what he wanted to do. Perhaps I should let him take care of getting the money back as he sees fit. I should stay out of it. This closure is for him anyway. My only fear is that Sergio might not be willing to hand over the earnings so easily. If that happens, Teddy has no idea how to manage an immediate threat of violence or danger. I may have to be more involved than I initially thought. I will talk this over with Teddy on the ride over and figure out our plan for what needs to happen and play out.

Whatever happens, this will undoubtedly be a turning point in our lives. This particular meeting will mark the end of my immoral behavior.

CHAPTER 17

I only take one step outside into the downfall of snow and want to turn around. The whirling and twisting of the violent storm engulf me. The shrieking wind angrily whips the flakes all around. The nagging whirlwinds sting the little-exposed skin on my cheeks. I feel the need to surrender to a warmer shelter as quickly as I can because this is extremely uncomfortable.

Teddy sits in the same Civic that I left him in yesterday to pursue the death-bound Marco. The car sits a mere thirty feet or so away, but through the harsh weather and fresh accumulation of snow, this is no cakewalk. Teddy called me as soon as he arrived so that I did not have to wait out in the cold. The rest of the scenery is hard to make out due to the thick whiteness distorting the view. The only reason I can see him out here waiting is that the lights are shining from his headlights.

As soon as I grasp the handle, I throw the car door open and jump in quickly. With my second move, I grab the inside of the door and slam it shut. The heater has been on for some time, so the interior of the vehicle is significantly warmer than the outdoor environment. I push my raw face close to the heater to warm it up.

"Holy Shit!" I say. "It has got to be well under zero degrees out there. I'm pretty sure I have never seen it this cold before."

"Yeah," Teddy agrees, "I've finally been able to defrost the window after taking care of that work outside. This weather has just been getting worse and worse. I don't know what is going on."

I decide to steer the conversation away from the weather and go straight to the serious matter of the moment.

"Before I left, I grabbed my gun and went to the drawer to get one for you. I noticed that it wasn't there. Do you have it with you?"

"Yeah, I do," Teddy says. "I have been feeling uncomfortable over the last day or so and decided to keep it on me at all times. Is that okay?"

I remember that he had it close to him earlier when we ate and was reaching for it when I came back from being with Marco. He has been a little paranoid recently and kept the gun nearby.

"That's why I offered it to you yesterday," I tell him. "It's completely fine with me."

Teddy nods, takes the weapon out, and lays it in his hands. He stares down at the cold metal and begins to study it.

"We aren't going to use these tonight, are we?" he asks me, looking up to my eyes.

"No, Teddy, I don't intend to," I say. "I only want you and me to have these for protection. I know how uncomfortable you feel about killing, and I don't intend for you to start. If everything works out the way it should, we will be able to get the money and get out of there quickly without complications. I'm serious about my new stance on life. I'm done being this awful person. Sergio doesn't need to die, nor does he deserve a dead brother. For that matter, he doesn't even deserve the robbery that we are about to pull on him. I'm only doing this for you, and only you, Teddy. If you want to back out now, I will happily oblige. So… Do you really want to go through with this now?"

Without thinking twice, he answers, "Yes, I need to. This has to be done, Kev. Despite your feelings, my thoughts haven't changed on the subject. I have never felt so strongly about something."

"Alright," I surrender. I then jump right into strategizing. "Now let me discuss our plan while you drive us over there. You know where you're going, right?"

"Yeah," he says. "The directions aren't too hard. His place is only about twenty to twenty-five miles from here. It is a pretty short ride if we can make it through this snow."

"Well, let's get going then," I tell him. "Be careful with these road conditions, though. I don't want us spinning out and getting into an accident. The last thing we want is any police involvement."

Teddy shifts the vehicle into drive and begins to pull out of the parking lot. The windshield wipers have been set on high to compete with the persistent snowfall on the window. I feel the soft snow crunching under our tires as our engine pushes us through it.

"This is really gonna be it then, huh?" Teddy asks. "This is the last time we'll ever see Sergio. All those long years we spent with the Celettas. Now it is just us. I know we talked about this earlier, but why exactly do you think they decided to turn on us like that? I have constantly been thinking about this but still can't put a finger on it. After all we've been through together, why now?"

I also had plenty of time to think over the last day or so, but I do not have many answers either. I have internally speculated and only seem to have part of the picture. What drove them to make such a bold move against us? What was that turning point? Did getting a little more money out of the deal really outweigh our lifelong friendships?

I recall the most recent conversations that I had with the Celettas. The way they acted or the discussions we had do not point to any clues or indication that something was off. I am drawing a blank. There is no way that their decision was made overnight. This thought brings me back to the internal reflections I had at the storage unit. Maybe just like me, the slow corruption of their morals over the years finally allowed them to choose a darker path.

"I think that all of us have gone so far down the path of freedom from responsibility that our judgment is skewed," I tell him. "I think that they didn't want to split the money four ways. By getting rid of us, they essentially doubled their returns. We haven't cared for anyone else's problems that were caused by our greed and ambition. It was only a matter of time until we stopped caring for those in our own group too. Do you see what I've been trying to tell you? What we've been doing for the last couple of years has slowly been turning us into monsters. None of us can think straight anymore. We've become so ingrained in this criminal mindset that it has dictated our lifestyle and molded us into who we are now."

"I don't know about that," Teddy promptly responds. "I think that you might be reaching a bit with that conclusion. I have a hard time believing that the Celettas transformed into this. I know that they have been our friends for a long time, but do you think they have always placed the group's interests over their own? I think we probably just trusted them too much. When they realized over time that they could make a move on their own, they decided to take it. I think we just teamed up with the wrong people, Kev. I know that they've been our friends for who knows how long, but did you always trust them? Did you think that they would stick by your side forever? I don't know about you, but I think that they could have turned on us at any point. They didn't suddenly become greedy. That is who they are, and it has finally surfaced."

Teddy's rebuttal to my theory actually made some sense. Perhaps I was wrong and gave them the benefit of the doubt. Teddy and I had a stronger relationship with each other than either of us had with the two of them. They also trusted each other more than Teddy and me. Something about this situation is not quite right, though. If our coordination was so smooth, and our robbery tactics so refined, why do their own thing now? Even from a financial standpoint, they had to know that the long-term success of working together outweighed a one-time boost in payout profit.

"Whatever the reasoning," Teddy continues, "I want to prove to Sergio that I will not be a pushover. You know that I've been on the butt end of the Celettas' abuse for years because of my younger age and fear of violence. It is time to stand up for myself."

As he spoke, he kept his eyes on the road ahead, probably to study the terrain through the declining visibility.

I cannot argue with Teddy's viewpoint. It just feels wrong stealing from a man who lost his brother. Teddy felt like this was a kind of retribution, though. A reparation for Sergio's decision to cut us out.

A sharp pain suddenly pierces through the swollen lump on my head. I instinctively caress it to assess the wound.

"You need to tell me this plan, man," he anxiously shoots. "What do you want me to do?"

The truth is that I would need some time to figure out the best way to go about it. Teddy's phone call woke me up not that long ago, so I did not have enough of a heads up to think about it. I will just have to tell him on the spot what I think the best approach should be.

"So, he thinks we are holding Marco hostage?" I ask him.

"Yeah," he affirms.

"First of all, that is pretty messed up," I say. "Secondly, he is quickly going to realize that Marco isn't with us at all. He is expecting us, too, so there is a significant chance that he is armed and waiting. He might've backed down and easily given us the money if Marco was with us, but because this isn't the case, he might be frustrated and not willing to hand it over so easily. You don't happen to know the layout of this building, do you? Any information or detail will be helpful."

"Unfortunately, I do not know, nor did I ask," Teddy answers. "But he did give me the address to his place. Also, the room number that he gave me is 15 if that helps. That's all I have."

"I'm assuming that this is an apartment or motel, so I'm going to need you to park farther away," I tell him. "I don't want him to see us coming in. We won't be able to make too much of a scene if there are people around. A quick escape in this type of weather will be impossible. We are going to need to negotiate the terms for the money. Problem is, we really don't have anything to negotiate with."

I wait before I continue to speak and think about the situation. How can we get this money from Sergio? The answer is obvious, but I worry that Teddy would be unfit to do the job.

"You will need to surprise him," I continue. "Catch him off guard and use the threat of violence to force him to yield to our needs. It's what we've always done in our robberies over the years. You will somehow need to sneak up on him because he will be expecting us. Due to your history of non-violent behavior, you are not considered a threat or enforcer in his eyes. This will be a tough task with quite a bit of variability in what could potentially happen. Are you up to this, even with all the risk?"

"I will be," he affirms, sticking to his decision yet again.

"Okay then," I say. "Let's get over there and make it happen."

As much as I do not convey it to him, I am not comfortable with all the risks and uncertainty we will face. The odds that everything will work out the way we want it to are pretty slim. A startled Sergio could easily kill a passive or unsure Teddy. A nervousness begins to build in my lower stomach.

Teddy continues to keep his head straight forward on the road and has not glanced over at me for some time. He is worried too. Though he has been in threatening situations before, this one is a lot different. This time Teddy has to be in charge. This has to be his moment.

Teddy seems quite different from the young boy I used to know. I am not sure if the shortened haircut has anything to do with it or if it is from the stress on his body over the last couple of days, but it is apparent to me. The fresh skin of his forehead is now visible and is slightly whiter because it has not seen the sun in several years.

"We're just about there," Teddy says. "It is only about one more mile out."

"Wow! That seems pretty quick," I say. "It must be because it is pretty much a straight shot. I think we've turned like twice this entire time. Pretty funny how close Sergio actually was to us, huh Ted?"

He gives a slight nod.

"Here's the deal. We're going to have to pull off the side of the road before we get there. Pull off before we pass the last set of trees so they can block the view of our car. I can see the end of the trees up ahead. Make sure you turn off the car and the lights."

He nods again.

Teddy does as I tell him, parking our Civic on the side of the road with the trees blocking our view from the building up ahead. He kills the engine and lights.

"We're here," he says, finally turning to look over at me.

"You okay?" I ask. "You're starting to look pretty uptight."

He really is. The stern look on his face makes me uncomfortable.

"Yeah, I think so," he says, looking right at me.

His uneasiness overwhelms his ability to hide it. His heavy breathing with the fearful look in his eyes tells me all I need to know. As much as Teddy "has" to do this, he cannot bring himself to do it. This is not who he is, and it should not have to be.

"Let's just go back," I tell him. "This is just too much. We're getting carried away with what is going on. Let's just relax and get some sleep so we can return to some sense of normalcy."

"You know that I can't do that," Teddy stares back at me. "I've already decided this. Tonight is for me."

I see terror, almost to the point of shock in his eyes. His breathing grows to that of borderline hyperventilation. He, too, cannot believe what he is about to do.

There is no way that I can let him go through with this. His terrified demeanor tells me that he is not ready. I fear that he poses a danger to himself. If I let Teddy encounter Sergio by himself, the situation could go downhill fast. I care too much for Teddy. I cannot let him do it. He is my best friend, my brother. I have to look out for his best interests. Since he is unwilling to listen to me and give up this idea, there is only one thing I can do now. I do not wish to do this, but it is the only way to protect him.

"Teddy," I offer my idea, "you stay here and let me do this. I'll go in and take care of this on my own."

"No!" Teddy says. "This is my thing. I need to do it. I don't want you to have to take care of me all the time. I have to do this for myself. I need to show Sergio who I am."

"I'll do it for you," I say. "I've always looked out for you, and I don't mind doing so. I know that we are so much older now, and you want this for yourself, but now is not the right time. After this, we will be able to get away from this worthless kind of life. Your new life is where you should become your own man, not at the end of this one. I'll do this for you now, and after this, that's it. This life of destruction is over."

Teddy just continues to watch me. He did not know how to answer. Deep down, I know that he wants me to do this instead of him.

"Alright," Teddy finally sighs, relieved. "I'll stay here. You'll be better at this than me anyway. You're smart in these situations. I appreciate you always being there for me."

"I got you, man," I say. "Don't worry about it. I wouldn't be comfortable sending you in there to do this anyway. It would kill me. Let me go in there, talk to Sergio, and we can get out of here. We'll be done with it."

I can see both the appreciation and relief in Teddy's expression. "It has been nice having such a great friend like you," he replies. "I can't say that about everyone, but knowing someone like you has really opened my eyes. I know that you're troubled by the mistakes of your past, but you do have a good heart."

"Thanks Teddy," I say. "That does mean a lot to me."

I look out into the fierce blizzard that I am about to venture through in a few moments. The climate outside is not as forgiving as both of our attitudes inside this Honda Civic. I must fight through this last challenge ahead of me to earn the honorable existence that I thirst to embrace.

I stuff my pistol under my jacket. I hate that I have it, but it will be necessary to have in my negotiation with Sergio. It will be used merely as a tool, not the fatal weapon that it was created to be. I have to promise myself it this time.

"I'm heading out," I say. "I'll see you in a few."

"Good luck!" he says as I open the door and jump out into the storm.

CHAPTER 18

The flurries of endless whiteness hurriedly push themselves to the ground. Flakes are not falling individually but instead are clustered together to increase their descent to the earth. They drop angrily, violently screaming as they shoot from the sky. I cover my face to defend it from the fierce biting of the rogue factions.

I step off the side of the road into the knee-deep snow. I forcefully shuffle and kick through the deep pile to move forward. The row of trees that shields our car from view is probably not necessary. I can barely see three feet in front of me through this mixture of darkness and concentrated snowfall. After several strides, I turn around and can hardly see the car that I left just moments ago.

I travel past the last few trees. Though I cannot see it, ahead of me is the building where Sergio resides. I see no light, nor can I even make out the silhouette of the building. I continue moving ahead toward the middle of this snow-globed field, trusting that if I cannot see him, there is no way that he can see me.

The insulation in my boots is not bad, but the constant trudging through the crunchy snow makes my toes feel colder and colder with every movement. The elements are clearly resentful of the intrusion of my warm body into their environment.

As I continue moving in the direction of where I think this building should be, I still see no light. I find it strange that I do not see any form of illumination, even through the thick snowfall. Could Teddy be wrong about the location? Or could this be a trap that Sergio has planned? Sergio is an intelligent guy. The opportunity to surprise us and take back his brother has probably crossed his mind. But perhaps I am wrong. Maybe this snow has just shielded my view significantly. Regardless, I force my foot forward again through this growing pile to see what Sergio has in store for me.

With every second that passes, my extremities increasingly grow numb. I have only been out here for two minutes, and it is already getting to me. I do not think there is any way that my body can take being out here for more than five more minutes. Also, the physical exertion through these mounds has already exhausted me.

My eyes finally catch a glow out in the distance ahead. It is meager in size and is the only light that I can see. I continue moving toward it.

Excitement jolts through me. Sergio must be here.

The dim, amber color comes from inside a window above a door. As I draw nearer, I begin to see the outline of the building surrounding the light. The building must be at least a hundred yards in length, with six doors evenly spaced across it. The only light that I see comes from above the second door from the left. I direct my movements toward this second door. I do not fear Sergio seeing me because the window above the door is too high. It would be impossible to see anyone in these blizzard-like conditions anyway.

The fact that only one light is on perplexes me. If this is a motel, should the entire building be illuminated? Even though it is the middle of the night, most commercial overnight establishments tend to keep their lights on to attract more customers.

As I get closer, the answer becomes clear. The darkened paint that is chipping off the building contrasts with the bright graffiti that litters the exterior. Pieces of brick are missing, and some of the paneling is warped or deformed. I reach the front of the second door and notice its coarse wood is splintering. This building has been vacant for quite some time.

It is hard to tell, but this place does not appear to be a motel or apartment complex. It seems like this building was leased to various businesses for office space at some point. All of those ventures must have moved out long ago.

I stop in front of the door and take a look around. A weathered sign on the left side indicates *Rooms 11-20*. Teddy was correct about the room number. Sergio has not thrown any sort of curveball at me just yet.

From the looks of the abandoned structure, Sergio is probably the only one in residence unless, of course, any homeless have found shelter here. This confrontation will only involve the two of us. My nervousness escalates to fear. I do not have a plan B, nor do I have anyone to back me up now. It is just me. If Sergio is going to pull something, I must react quickly.

"This is it, this is it," I repeat softly to myself. The end of this is near.

Wasting my time out in the cold will do nothing but postpone the event and have me needlessly think about it. I take one last look behind me to see if I can catch a glimpse of the trees hiding Teddy's vehicle. The attempt is in vain, though, as all I can see is mere blackness and the maniacal twisting of snow. "This is for you, my brother," I say to him quietly through the darkness.

I pull out my pistol, silently grasp the rusted handle on the door, and press it open swiftly, yet carefully, as to make as little noise as possible. As I push, the strength of the enraged storm overwhelms my grip and thrusts the door into the inside wall with a powerful *BANG!*

I force my weapon ahead of me to take aim as soon as I realize the door is opening on its own. So much for a silent entry. Luckily, this door leads to a hallway with no one directly inside. Three faint light fixtures align the ceiling of the hall. I can barely see the five doors lined up on both sides.

"Marco?" I hear from one of the distant rooms down the hall, "Is that you?"

The voice is definitely Sergio's. The noise created by the smacking door has gotten his attention. I hurriedly slide through the corridor toward his words, keeping my footsteps light as to suppress the sound of my approach. I ignore the shrieking wind from the doorway behind as I continue. I catch a glimpse of the door numbers on the left. Rooms eleven through fifteen should be on this side. Sergio's room will be the last one on the left if he is indeed in number 15 like Teddy said.

I reach the last door, and sure enough, the aging wooden number validates my assumption.

"Teddy!?" he tries again. "Is that you?"

Wrong again, I think to myself. He has no idea what is coming.

With a fear of waiting too long without responding, causing a recently startled Sergio to become more cautious, I decide to make my move. With my hand gripped firmly around my weapon, I shove my shoulder into the door to break into Sergio's room.

CHAPTER 19

I enter with my pistol facing forward, ready to direct my aim to Sergio's position in the room. I immediately witness his form in the opposite corner sitting behind a desk, frantically rummaging inside it, probably for his weapon.

"Get those hands up!" I aggressively scream, thrusting my pistol toward him for emphasis.

With an instant realization of defeat, he gives up the search and shoves his hands into the air signaling a complete surrender. The look of shock fills his face with his eyes wide open and his eyebrows lifted to the peak of his forehead.

Since the immediate threat of danger has diminished, I pause for a few moments to study Sergio. The young man I knew all my life seems to have aged twenty years over the last day or so. The confidence that once lit up his face that made him appear strong and impenetrable is gone. It is now replaced with an air of hopelessness, giving the impression of being weathered and beaten from failed experiences. A paleness as white as a ghost covers the entirety of his face with a sickly weakened look. Even his pitch-dark hair seems to have faded and has speckles of gray throughout. His appearance takes me by surprise. It takes one or two looks for me to confirm that this is indeed the Celetta brother. Did his worry for Marco affect him to this extent?

After we try to read each other, Sergio suddenly breaks the silence, "I can't believe it. This really is the end, isn't it?"

"I didn't come here with the intent to kill," I say. "I wouldn't fear that unless you do something stupid. I only wish to retrieve the money that you took. It's mine now."

I instruct him to get up carefully and locate the hidden funds. I continue pointing my gun just in case he decides to make any sudden movements for a weapon. I do not fear any conflict, though, as his demeanor while getting up resembles that of surrender. His shoulders are slumped and his head hangs down. Sergio moves to a filing cabinet only a couple feet away from the desk and opens a drawer second from the top. Without a word, he pulls out a pack exactly resembling one used in the robbery and tosses it to me.

I unzip the pouch in my lap using my left hand and confirm that the contents are indeed all the cash that was taken. It includes the stacks from the safe and the Ziplocs of money collected from the teller stations. This transaction is seemingly uncomplicated and a lot easier than I first expected. No emotion of hate or rage fills me as I watch Sergio. I actually feel a certain amount of pity toward him as he moves in stooped resignation. Even though he decided to betray us, the retribution for his mistake far outweighs the punishment he deserves. I accomplished what I set out to do. I cannot think of anything appropriate to say to Sergio for the last time, so I determine that I should probably just go.

"Tell me where your gun is, Sergio," I say, deciding to grab his weapon before my departure. "I'll be on my way, and you'll never see nor hear from me again. That's all I have to say to you."

Before doing so, he looks right at me with those solemn brown eyes, pauses, and asks me the question: "Do you know where Marco is?"

I stop at his inquiry, wishing that I could have gotten out of here before he asked it. I look into those focused eyes and am at a loss for words. I cannot lie to him, but how do I break the news to him? I have to tell it to him straight, no matter the devastation that this disclosure will undeniably bring.

"You see..." I stop, gain my composure and start over.

"Things went wrong," I say, "and he's gone now."

"What do you mean?" he says, changing his demeanor to that of boldness and complete seriousness.

"I mean that he is gone forever now," I answer.

Sergio stands frozen in his spot, not moving or breathing. He is hit by a realization that he did not expect. He is shocked because he never considered that this could happen. Never again would he have a conversation with his little brother or have a relationship as close and unique. He now lives alone in a world with no direction, understanding, or purpose. His trademark resiliency is broken. Sergio is a defeated man.

Without any discernible movement, a steady stream begins to flow from his left eye. Following that one stream, several more tears start rolling down his face. He does not sniffle or verbally cry, but the tears alone tell me enough about his despair.

It would be too easy to tell Sergio that I regret what I did to Marco, but that would not do him justice. He would not want to hear such a thing from me anyway. I used to sit and think about my destructive behavior and how it related to my own moral being. As I witness this individual who has always been strong and emotionally stable break down before my eyes, that does not matter anymore. This morality struggle should never have been about me but instead about those who have been hurt by me. While I can change my thoughts and actions, I cannot fix nor restore the permanent damage that has been done. Many lives will forever be ruined as a direct result of my wrongdoing. Expressing my remorse cannot undo the past and restore happiness to those affected. All I can do moving forward is to avoid inflicting any more pain. I should leave things as they are because I cannot fix them. Any further action on my part would be damaging, no matter the sincerest of intentions.

I can hear Sergio start to breathe again with increasing strength and frequency. I look up at him and realize his tears have subsided and he is firmly clenching his teeth. His brown eyes have cleared and now stare piercingly into mine.

"You killed my brother, didn't you?" he says bluntly.

All of a sudden, a rush of worry floods me. I am in a place I do not want to be with Sergio's increasing anger. Any rash or inappropriate word choice will entice the emotionally-stricken Sergio to come at me, no matter if I am holding this gun or not.

"You killed Marco, didn't you?" he says again, already knowing the answer. "You killed your good friend, my little brother, you bastard! You are so damn cruel and sick!"

His eyes widen, and he begins huffing like a wolf about to strike its prey.

"How could you do that?" he screams.

I am stuck, scrambling for the words, hell, any words that might explain my actions.

"How could you do that!" he now shrieks, diving toward his desk.

"NO!" I yell with my weapon outstretched, "Stop that or I'll shoot you!"

"Shoot me then, you murderer!" he cries, scavenging for something in the desk.

Despite my previous proficiency in reacting quickly and instinctively, I stand frozen with my finger on the trigger and am unable to pull it. Even as he finds his gun, reaches over the desk and aims it in my direction, I stand rooted with my finger still. I see the flash from his first shot and close my eyes as I hear three ear-deafening booms discharge.

I keep my eyes shut, and all goes silent. The silence continues. Is the quietness due to the post-ringing from the shots, or is this lack of sound one of the experiences of death? I finally force myself to open my eyes. Sergio has his head down in his arms and appears to be weeping with the gun lying next to him. I look across my arms and chest and realize that none of his shots have hit me. I glance at the back wall and see all three bullet holes. In his fury, Sergio had been too passionate and impulsive to aim accurately, and this accounted for the array of misfires.

I drop my arm to my side and loosen the grip on the gun. It slowly slides through my fingers onto the wooden floor with a *Plop*! It does not matter that he almost killed me. I do not care.

His face is buried in his hands as the soft sobbing continues. Coming here was a mistake despite Teddy's insistence. It was not right to kick the poor man while he was down. It was not just the money I took, but everything else I stole from him. I stole his friendship, his trust, and, most importantly, his brother. It no longer matters that he turned on me and left me to be arrested. I probably deserved it for all the things I have done. Besides, the days of getting away with my crimes were probably limited anyway. Perhaps it would have been best if I had been caught and taken away to prevent this final infliction of suffering. Being locked up would not have just benefited society, but me as well. My freedom only allowed me to continue on such a heinous path.

I have done nothing but inflict hardship on all of my friends. I have hurt each of them in irreparable ways that no true friend ever should.

Poor Marco. His young soul was taken by my vengeful malice. He had no choice, nor was he aware that our final conversation in the car would be his last. He was a good kid despite the misdemeanors we persuaded him to get involved. He loved me as a brother for years and would never have fathomed the fate he would succumb to by my hand.

Poor Teddy. For years he has ignorantly looked up to me as such a righteous and absolute role model, while in reality, my actions and wrongdoings have contaminated his innocent nature. He has listened and followed so closely that he never questioned my murders, quest for retribution, or even the initial onset of criminal activity. He followed me with a blind devotion that proved more damaging than he or I could have ever imagined.

Poor Sergio. As I stand here watching the wretched man who used to be so capable and unyielding, I feel my own eyes begin to fill. My heart sinks, and the tears swell to such a point that they cannot hold. I let them go as both Sergio and I sob simultaneously with intervals of sniffling. What have I done?

"I'm so sor... sorr... sorry, Sergio," I cry. "I kn.. know that nothing I c... can say or do will make things better or bring him back, but I just want to t... tell you that."

Sergio does not look up or even catch that I am talking to him. His anguish has brought him to a new level of misery where he is completely unaware of his surroundings.

For minutes we sit, both lost in our grief. We have no plan of what to do next, nor do we even care at this point. I come to the realization that I cannot do this to Sergio. I cannot rob this poor man again. I have already taken too much. The money is not a big deal at all. He will need it more than Teddy and I.

"Here," I say, putting the pouch on his desk and pushing it forward. "Keep this! I don't want it anymore. It is yours."

Sergio looks up through his watery eyes and takes a few moments to figure out what I am doing. "I don't want it," he says. "Take it and get out of here. Let me be."

"I do not want to make a big deal of this," I say, "but I think that you'll need it more than me. Take it, and you'll never see nor hear from me again."

Sergio stares at the bag, trying to decide what he wants to do with it. After some thought, he leans across the table and softly pulls it back over to him.

"I have to go," he says, "I cannot stay here anymore. I can't deal with it here. I have to leave now."

"I understand," I say earnestly. "I think that is how it'll have to be."

Sergio stands up, throws the bag over his shoulder, and pushes his gun across the desk. "I don't need this anymore."

He crosses the room to the hallway door and opens it.

With no words to correct my past wrongdoings or misguided actions, I tell him the only two words that I can.

"Goodbye Sergio," I say to him.

He looks back and gives me one last glance before he leaves the room. It is not a glance of respect, but one that signifies a "goodbye" response. It is a moment that officially puts to rest the summation of our friendship and long history together. The last look in those soft, shiny eyes, in complete contrast with his rugged face and stature, brings this final chapter of our lives to an end.

As he shuts the door behind him, I reflect on all the games, laughs, smiles, and years of fun that I shared growing up with both he and Marco. We had some great times in those early days, where innocence and happiness were all that we knew.

The Bad Guy

CHAPTER 20

BANG! *BANG!* The sound instantly rips through my ears and makes me jump unexpectedly. What was that? The thoughtful experience with Sergio quickly vanishes from my mind. I bend down to grab the pistol that I dropped earlier and creep slowly to the door that Sergio exited just seconds ago. With this sudden emergence of confusion, I have to see what happened before I make a move.

I grasp my hand onto the cold knob and take a big breath before cracking the door open. I gently nudge the door a few inches and peek around the corner to get a view of the hallway. I gasp at the scene.

I adjust from my cautionary position and stand up straight as I push the door open to enter into the hallway. In a million years, I never would have envisioned the sight in front of me. I drop the gun to my side as I become filled with grief and hopelessness. Things have gotten way out of hand these last couple of days, and it is all over now.

Sergio's body lies there in the middle of the hallway floor. Two bullet holes pierced his midsection. Blood is rapidly soaking his sweater and the carpeted floor around him. He just lies there, dead. The pouch of money is still under his arm, the money that was the source of all our problems, the money that we all could not share as a group.

I move my eyes to the end of the hallway toward the entrance of the building. There he stands, gun in hand, still pointing down at the victim whose life he just took. Teddy shot down the defenseless Sergio as he was trying to leave.

I become puzzled. Teddy would not hurt a fly, much less kill a man. Not just that, but the man that he killed was one of his best friends.

A nefarious smirk crosses Teddy's face as he gazes down upon Sergio's lifeless body. I have never seen this type of expression or reaction to anything remotely violent in Teddy's character. Fear streams through my veins. Everything I thought I knew about Teddy has drained from my comprehension. Who is this person in front of me?

"He almost escaped from you," Teddy breaks the silence. "I made sure that he did not make it too far, though." He gives a short chuckle following the sly remark.

Teddy thought that Sergio was escaping and must have shot him to avoid us losing both him and the money. I need to explain to him what just transpired between Sergio and me and why I decided to let him go. My heart breaks at the way all of this has unraveled. Had Teddy known, Sergio would be alive right now. Teddy would also not have to bear the long-term regret of taking someone's life. It was not just anyone, either. It was Sergio.

"Damn it!" I have to break it to him, "I'm sorry that I could not tell you this immediately, but I decided that things would be best if I just let Sergio go. I talked to him in the room for a bit and could not let myself kill another person, especially a friend. I want to change. I have been haunted by my past for so long and cannot bear to be the person that I am any longer. Taking vengeance on him wasn't the answer. Sometimes you need to move on and let things be. I don't care about the money anymore. Screw the money. All I want is just a little bit of happiness. Killing him would have never given me peace. I regret the torture I've put all those people through, the families I've hurt, and all the pain I have caused. I'm sorry for all of it. I can't do this anymore. I wish that I could've let you know about these thoughts earlier. I'm so sorry, Teddy. He left his gun behind, and I let him leave. Had I told you about that, then Sergio would still be......"

Teddy is not paying any attention to me but instead continues to stare intently at the body on the floor. I would not be surprised, as he probably would be shocked at the taking of a life, but the crooked grin on his face does not fade. What is wrong with him?

His eyes then move up into mine. That smile scares me. Without any change in expression or posture, he promptly lifts the weapon and points it toward my head.

I instantly step back and freeze. What the hell is going on? My eyes become terror-stricken. My expression must resemble the look on those faces who have stared at my raised pistol. My brain is stuck. Complete words cannot escape from my mouth. I find myself sputtering nonsense trying to grasp the situation at hand. "Wha...why are you doing this?" finally emerges from my lips.

Time seems to stop as I move my eyes from the gun to Teddy. The look on his face is worn, but an angry fire from within him shows a determined, unmoving intention. I do not know what to do. I did not plan for my life to end right here, right now. Never have I seen a weapon look so menacing. A uselessness floods through me as despair withdraws all hope. I feel an instant desire to cry to dispel all of the anxiety and worry from my life. How did I get here? How did we get to this point?

My best friend wants me dead. The little guy I have watched grow up, and spent my whole life trying to protect, is standing in front of me ready to kill me now. Teddy always had my back, and I always had his. I cannot understand why he would do such a thing to me. He knows that I have continually looked out for him.

Unwavering, he finally answers my question. "You didn't know that I was in on Sergio's and Marco's plan, did you?"

"I don't understand," I respond, knowing full well that what he would say next would break my heart even further.

"You expressed to me that you believed that both Sergio and Marco were working together as brothers to keep the money that we obtained as a group. That, my friend, was never the case."

I made an assumption about Marco and Sergio and blindly accepted it. I should have asked Sergio before he left the room why he did what he did to me, but in the emotion of the moment, I just let him go. I figured that his answer would not make any difference. With Marco, my feelings were so fraught with anger and revenge, that any question like that would never have occurred to me. If I had just given Marco a moment to speak, I would have understood everything.

Teddy continues, "The three of us decided that the killing habit you adopted was too much for all of us to handle if we were to continue with our robberies. You are a smart guy, Kevin, but you are equally emotional and often get carried away by it. We figured the best way to let you go was by knocking you out at the bank, allowing the cops to take care of you there. You would've been their problem then. You would be confused and upset, but still too proud and loyal to me to rat us out to the police."

"Hold on!" I chime in, "first of all, why didn't you guys talk to me? I would've been rational if you guys had talked to me.

Secondly, you were also knocked out and then picked up by the cops. All three of you guys could not have been working together. They turned on you too!"

"Ha! Ha!" Teddy laughs at my declaration. "I'm not really sure how to answer the first part. Sergio and Marco came to a consensus that you would not be too fond of our opinion of you. They figured that you might get kinda hot-headed and perhaps pose a problem if we were to talk to you. I don't know too much about what they were thinking, though. It did not make much sense to me either. I can definitely enlighten you as to what truly happened at the bank, however. Do you see any nasty bruises or cuts on my head like the one on yours?"

Now that he mentions it, I do not notice or recall seeing any marks on his head that are as recognizable as the one upon my forehead. Even after he cut his hair the other day, I failed to realize that. If he had actually been knocked out, he certainly would have had some visible wound that he would have tended to in our motel room. I shake my head "no" to respond to his question.

"I was never knocked out at the bank," he says. "I lied to you about that. If I had been knocked out, why would I be handcuffed and put in the back of the cop car before you? I stayed in the back of the building because I didn't think I could take the sight of Sergio knocking you, my greatest friend, out in front of me. It was stupid, I know, but with the intensity of the situation, I didn't think I could handle witnessing you getting betrayed by us."

"So, what actually happened to you then? You just got caught?"

"I sure did!" he answers. "Those two cops swarmed in right after you got knocked out, and Marco, Sergio, and I all bolted for the vehicles. They were both lucky and were able to get to their vehicles and escape. I was not quite as lucky, though. As I raced through the parking lot, one of the cops jumped out of the police car and tackled me to the pavement. I was caught at that point."

How did I not consider this possibility? I was so enraged with Sergio and Marco over the last couple of days that I was not thinking clearly. The actual series of events during the robbery did not occur the way I thought they had.

"I sat in the police car," Teddy continues, "knowing far too well that my life of freedom was over. I did not regret my actions and what we had done because I knew what I had gotten myself into and had to pay the consequences. I was sitting in the back of the car with all of these thoughts going through my head when you, Mr. Hero, pulled a ridiculous stunt to hijack the car and save me. At that point, I knew I was free. There was no way in hell that I could've told you what truly happened after that. You were oblivious to the truth anyway. I could tell that all your energy was focused on blaming Sergio and Marco."

Everything starts falling into place, but the biggest question of all was still left unanswered.

"Why did you allow me to kill both Marco and Sergio, knowing that they really didn't deserve it? You were in on their plan, too. What made you do your own thing? You turned on me and then on them, you son-of-a-bitch!"

That smirk across his face grows so wide that it exposes his left canine tooth. The demonic smile and piercing eyes accentuate the threat of the weapon he eagerly aims at me.

"Careful," he says, snickering. "Don't get too excited. I have a gun in my hand."

He then begins to explain.

"Why would I have stopped you on your rampage against the Celetta brothers? I was going to have to share the money with them. I knew that with every person you killed, I would have more money in my hands. Call it greed or call it

166

backstabbing, I don't care. It is only business to me. I will need as much money as I can get anyway. The police know my face now. I won't be able to walk anywhere safely, much less attempt another robbery with confidence. I want, no, I need that money, Kev."

My heart sinks even lower. Teddy is not the person I intended him to be. I failed him throughout the years and wish I could take everything back now. I want him to be that innocent little boy. I want him to have a respectable job with a wonderful family. I want him to enjoy life and be happy, not killing friends for money and hiding from the police for the rest of his life. I undeniably failed him. I throw my face into my left hand, pressing my fingers solidly against my cheeks and over my eyes. I cannot believe this is happening.

"You think that you stumbled upon Marco by chance at lunch yesterday?" Teddy continues. "We all had each other's numbers in our cell phones before the robbery. We pre-planned it without you. I had access to them on my phone the entire time. Before you woke up yesterday morning, I called Marco and he was very willing to meet me at that gas station. I led him to believe that I was lucky to escape from the bank and was looking forward to meeting up with him and Sergio."

"You led me right to him?" I ask, trying to confirm the statement Teddy just divulged.

"Didn't Marco look like he was waiting for someone yesterday?" Teddy reveals. "He was standing there, waiting for someone. Waiting for me. I turned off my cell phone so it wouldn't ring because you might piece things together and realize he's calling me. He didn't expect to find you, an angry you, instead of me. Didn't quite work out for him too well, huh?"

Teddy knew exactly what I would do. He planned for me to kill Marco. He knew that would happen if I "randomly" found him in the most coincidental of circumstances. Teddy knew that there was no way that I was going to allow that golden opportunity to slip away from me. He even talked me into going out for a Christmas lunch. He knew I would pick the gas station. I picked it as though it was my idea. I played right into his game without even realizing it.

"And Sergio? How did you manage to find out that he was here? I am assuming that the 'urgent call' you made to me that woke me up wasn't entirely true."

"Yes, my friend, you are completely correct," Teddy affirms. "You remember that I was trying to talk you into following Marco back to Sergio when you found him yesterday? I figured it would be easier if you just killed them together. You confronted him instead, though, and murdered Marco by himself, so I had to come up with another plan. I went out to meet with a worried Sergio a few hours ago while I was 'supposedly' cleaning up the Marco mess for you. I called him and told him that I went to meet up with Marco earlier in the day, but he never showed up. Sergio and I then met up to discuss what might've happened to Marco. You should've seen him. He was overly paranoid. He was freaking out, saying that the cops probably knew exactly where we were and were just waiting for an opportune moment to pounce. He even mentioned that knocking you out was such a horrible idea and kept kicking himself about what he'd done. Sergio told me, 'I can't believe I would do such a thing to a good friend. What were we thinking? Karma is going to come back strong against us now. What a horrible mistake, what a bad day, why did this happen?' Blah blah blah! When I was about to leave, he asked if I wanted to stay over at this place with him. I told him sure, but I just needed to pick up a few things and would head over later. I called you soon after that to wake you up on my way back to the motel."

"So you knew where he was staying then, huh?" I ask.

"Yes," Teddy says to clarify. "I knew he was here in this place all along. I was supposed to come back here and stay with Sergio and Marco after the robbery, but you know that didn't work out as planned. The only reason that I went out with him earlier was so that he would expect me to be coming here, not you. Sergio inviting me to stay with him was all I needed. Since he was expecting me, I didn't want him to be too volatile when he heard you arrive. I was the one that allowed you to make the safe entry here. You didn't startle him too much coming in, did you?"

"I guess not," I acknowledge. "So you made up that bullshit story about negotiating to get me over here to do your dirty work. I didn't kill him as you expected, though."

"I was ready for that as you can see," he says as he nods his head down toward his outstretched pistol.

"How did you know that in my confrontations with Marco and Sergio that they wouldn't discuss your involvement and weed out your lies to me?" I ask.

"I did worry about that," he answers. "That's why I had the gun on me and was skeptical when you first arrived back from meeting with Marco. That is why I am here with this gun now. I knew that there was a chance you could learn the truth, but you were so emotional in both situations that you didn't bother to ask for it. There were so many things you could have asked them, and you chose not to. I appreciate you offering that extra weapon to me yesterday, or I would've never been able to follow through with this."

"Well, you got what you wanted, then," I say. "Two of your friends are dead and gone. So what happens next? What are you going to do with me?"

After I ask these questions, I instantly realize the answer. Teddy's demeanor is unchanging, and the weapon seems even more menacing. He does not intend for me to make it out of here.

"Oh Kevin, it has been a long ride and you have been such a great mentor and friend to me," he says. "It is unfortunate that it is going to have to end like this. A long time ago, you told me that I needed something to take everything out of life that I could. This is that something, that something that keeps me alive, it keeps me going. I am sick and tired of being the one that has to follow. I need my own direction. I need to do my own thing from now on, Kevin. You understand? This money is mine. It is way more important to me than it would have been to any of you. I need it to keep going."

Teddy is a monster. He is not that same little kid that used to be my friend. He has transformed into something horrible. My hands go numb, and that feeling begins moving up my forearms. My gun hangs limply at my side. My stomach clenches tightly and causes my body to shake. Tears start to stream down my face. I am going to die. Die by the hands of a friend. I imagine the bullet whizzing out from the barrel and straight into my brain before I would have a chance to comprehend what happened. My head already hurts from the realization that these are the last few moments that it will be together in one piece. My clock is ticking. I do not want to be shot mid-thought. Being in the middle of a thought process as I am shot in the head seems like it would be more painful. I am not ready to go just yet. There are still so many things to think, work out, experience, and do.

"Pleeease don't kill me!" I sob to Teddy. "You can't do this. I would never let anything happen to you! You are my little buddy. You always have been, and you always will be. There is no way this is happening. I love you, man. This cannot be it. Show me some mercy, show me some of the respect that I have shown to you."

I wipe the tears from my eyes and look directly into Teddy's. He remains unmoved by the pain he sees in me. The gun in his hand points perfectly in my direction without wavering. The crooked smile tarnishing his lips crushes all hope of any remorse. This is my ending.

"A good friend once told me," Teddy speaks in a solid tone, "be careful who you trust."

The gun holds steady in his hands as he pulls the trigger.

***

All falls silent except for the whooshing and whistling of the heavy winds that batter and throw themselves against the decrepit building. Teddy Lagutus regains his composure and steps carefully between the two bloodied bodies to retrieve the money pack under Sergio's lifeless arm. Following a short struggle to get the pack from under him, he promptly throws it around his own arm and turns around. After a few careful foot placements over the bodies and down the hall, Teddy walks through the open entrance door. Without any hesitation, he moves alone into the violent world as the ice immediately bites his face. He never turns around but instead continues moving forward into the cold, unforgiving, and unrelenting December night.